I0549839

Northwest Vignettes

Volume One

Creative Nonfiction Stories
by NW Writers

Selected by

Eckley Guerin
and
Patricia Williams

Moonlight
Garden

Cover art by Michael Dillon.

Some story art by Diantha Weilepp,
Mick Alderman, Agnes Brown, Cat Loyd,
and Rennee Hammons.

Edited by Caitlyn Schmidt, Eckley Pat Guerin, and S. C. Moore.

Published 2018, Moonlight Garden Publications, an imprint of Gazebo Gardens Publishing, LLC.
www.GazeboGardensPublishing.com

978-1-938281-60-0   (paperback)
978-1-938281-61-7   (e-book)

Library of Congress Control Number: 2017915321

Printed in the United States of America.

ACKNOWLEDGEMENTS

We would like to thank all the many fine writers and illustrators who made this book possible.

Our staff of half a dozen volunteers, including Patricia Williams and Lorraine Andriesian, collected, organized, and typed up the stories submitted for this collection and gathered illustrations.

Unfortunately, we had a run of bad luck. First, our very helpful courier, Bob Bohnke, moved out of state, then the remainder of our staff—either by accident or illness—left the project, until we were down to one volunteer, me.

Fortunately, Shelley C. Moore of Gazebo Gardens Publishing is the type of person who is willing to jump right in and offer assistance, advice, and information. We also share the same set of ethics and beliefs, so we work well together.

Luckily, I finally found three new volunteers to help me finish the project by reading through more story submissions, typing up stories, and creating illustrations: Jody Mumford, Rennee Hammons, and Cat Loyd. They helped me ready and send all the materials to Shelley, allowing our collection of short stories and illustrations to be published.

Finally, I would like to give a special thank you to Michael Dillon for allowing us to use his beautiful painting for the cover of this volume. Although sea lions are not endearing to the local fishermen, they are loved by many of the tourists who visit Astoria—especially the children.

The royalties from the sale of this book will be donated to the River Song Foundation, helping homeless animals in Astoria, Warrenton, and Seaside, Oregon.

Eckley Guerin

TABLE OF CONTENTS

This volume of short stories
is dedicated to Brian F. Harrison,
1947 - 2015,
archeologist, teacher, and author.

"We've got all the samples
that we need for DNA."

Eating Gertie

Brian F. Harrison

By the first of April, we had finished our project in Alaska filming the discovery and excavation of a mammoth near the Tanana River. A small female, not what the director wanted, but what our Inuit guides had found for us. We laid out the grid, did our magnetometry and ground-penetrating radar, and excavated for the camera a mammoth we already knew was there.

We tried not to giggle as we peered earnestly eyeball-to-lens and explained how the techniques of modern science had prevailed over the expanse of the tundra, even penetrating the permafrost to locate the Ice Age mammal.

With the filming ended, and the equipment packed away in trunks, we waited for our usual dinner of Dinty Moore beef stew, barely warmed over a camp stove. The producer had screwed up the budget for getting us all by helicopter to the dig site, and we had to buy our own grub en route in Fairbanks.

A case of stew and one of canned peaches in heavy syrup were our meals for the entire two weeks. We were cranky about it. This should've been our last night of that crap, and tomorrow night we would be eating real food in Anchorage.

So we sat around the folding table, drinking Jack Daniels and talking about food the way hungry people do. Though it was late evening, it was still light out, and the mosquitoes were fierce. Our conversation was punctuated word for word by slaps. The stories of lobster, steaks, and salads made our mouths tingle. Even Emily's vegetarian lasagna fantasies caused stomach-shivers. So we talked of steaks and baked potatoes with sour cream and chives and bacon bits, drinking our whiskey and imagining a real meal on ceramic plates and real coffee after. An obsession it was, orgasmic fantasies of food.

It was Paul Dunbar, who had done the necropsy on the mammoth we'd dubbed Gertie, who got us started. "You know," he said, "we could have steaks tonight."

We all grumbled that he was a scoundrel to be talking like that when all we faced was more stew and peaches.

"Nope," he continued. "We could do it. Gertie's been dead for 12,000 years, but frozen all that time. We've got all the samples that we need for DNA, pathology, histology—the whole schmear. The rest of her is headed for UAF (University of Alaska Fairbanks) tomorrow. They're stripping her down for a bone exhibit."

Bob Frost, our cameraman, said, "But wouldn't they notice big chunks missing?"

"Nope. When they macerate the corpse, they'll chop off some hunks for later analysis, but they're hot for the skeleton."

Someone asked if there were parasites we should worry about, like trichinosis.

"I don't think so," replied a pathologist named Freeman. "We've studied it hard this week, to the point of doing everything twice for the damn camera, and didn't see any vermin in the muscle tissue. It's carnivores you have to be careful about eating."

More booze, more questions, and a general agreement was reached. Thus, Gertie came to be not only a scientific specimen, but our dinner plan.

Freeman and I walked to the cold shed where the carcass was being stored, and he took a pathology knife from a sheath under his parka.

I asked, "Where do we start carving?"

He pointed to Gertie's handsomely rounded haunch

and honed the blade. Pushing aside the guard hairs and pelt, he sliced through a layer of fascia and fat, peeling back layer by layer in an excavation of the flesh. At the muscle itself, he carved out a block of tissue then sliced that into steaks, cutting against the grain. I stood there, catching the meat on a lab tray, thinking this must be illegal or unscientific or something. But he worked with such surgeon's skill and confidence, I trusted he knew what he was doing.

I turned to carry the meat out to the fire pit, but Derek stopped me.

"Wait, Brian." With his knife, he deftly severed the flesh of the soft underbelly and cut into the stomach. Reaching in with latex-gloved hands, he scooped out what, to me, looked like spinach: the half-digested moss and lichens of the mammal's last supper. "Vitamins," he said with a rare twinkle.

We carried the plates of raw meat and a side dish of vegetables to the campfire, where equipment pallets had become red-hot coals. Our griddle was a sheet of steel fortuitously fallen off a gas chromatograph, now greased with mammoth fat. The greenery went into the stew pot, where it bubbled like a hot pool at Yellowstone.

The meat sizzled as it seared on the makeshift grill, ice crystals exploding in the suet. After a few minutes, I ladled helpings onto everyone's plate, except for Emily, who had only the cooked greens with a bit of salt.

We looked up into the Sony Digital's lens when the narrator began his spiel. "A sight unseen on this endless tundra for a hundred centuries, men savoring the roasted flesh of a mammoth under the midnight sun..."

Everyone laughed, and our chief scientist, Dr. Pound, tapped his tin cup for attention. He was getting tipsy and tapped it a bit hard, spilling some of the grape juice fortified by ethanol from the chemical stores.

Ignoring the spreading purple stain, he squinted carefully, looking around the table, then up into the mountains glowing in the frigid twilight. "Father Darwin," he intoned, "Agassiz, Stephen Jay Gould, the

Leakey Family, and all the other saints, bless this Pleistocene fauna we share tonight in your revered names."

"Amen," we agreed, and sat up to eat our supper.

Brian F. Harrison was born in 1947 in Spokane, Washington. He earned a Bachelor of Arts in Sociology in 1969 and a Master of Arts in Sociology in 1971, both from Gonzaga University.

Brian taught at St. Mary's College in Leavenworth, Kansas, and then worked as Parks and Recreation Director in Newport, Oregon, before being hired by Clatsop Community College in Astoria, Oregon, in 1978 to teach anthropology and sociology. During the summers, he worked as an archeologist, excavating at sites in Oregon, Washington, Alaska, Wales, Peru, and Easter Island. He continued his enthusiasm for learning after retirement through online courses in genetics, microbiology, and archeology.

An avid writer, Brian authored two books of poetry, Landscapes of Memory *and* Winter Companions, *a novel,* Chasing Shadows, *and numerous magazine and journal articles on archaeology and science. Harrison also appeared in two archaeology documentaries on the Discovery Channel.*

In 2015, Brian passed away and is survived by his wife, Margie, two sons, two grandsons, three sisters, and numerous nieces, nephews, and cousins.

"Pops, the one thing I want more than anything else is Ruby."

Ruby

Jonathan Guthrie

Mildred Wilhelm visited with Walter Anderson nearly every day at his home on the Oregon coast. On nice afternoons, when sun sifted through the palm fronds to dapple the lawn of the Sea View Retirement Residence, Mildred and Walter would stroll outside to sit in wicker chairs shaded by an umbrella and cooled by the breeze while they stared out at Haystack Rock.

"I like it better outdoors," Mildred would say to Walter. "It's nice in the home, but everything is so very, very antiseptic. Right down to the white shoes on the nurses' feet. Do you like white, Walter?"

Walter would purse his lips, not looking at Mildred. His gaze would move beyond where the gardener manicured flowerbeds to the beach. He would study the waves chasing each other across the sand. He would consider the clouds spooned onto the horizon like whipped cream. He would watch the seagulls performing high-wheeling acrobatics.

Then, having pretended all the while to ponder Mildred's question with great care, Walter would answer. "I suppose white is a satisfactory color, Mildred. Your hair is white. I like your hair very much. But for most things, I prefer red. Bright red. Like apples in an autumn orchard."

"Or the red of a ruby, Walter?"

"Why yes, Mildred. I like ruby red best of all."

Walter would fold himself into the cushions of the wicker chair, searching for a more comfortable position. His toes would wiggle inside his velvet slippers, and his hands would lace together as though in prayer.

When everything was in order, Walter would ask, "Did I ever tell you about Ruby, Mildred?"

Mildred would smile and say, "Perhaps. But I would enjoy hearing the story again, Walter."

Walter would nod and look away, not wanting Mildred to see him blink back the tears. For a long while, he would pretend to be engrossed in something, perhaps watching a distant ship tightrope walking the horizon. Finally, he would close his eyes and sigh, and the story would begin.

On a day that would be so different, Walter began the story, as always, by recalling the tragedy of his wife, Mary, dying during childbirth. His frail voice faltered for just a heartbeat as he told how he knelt at the bedside to kiss tender lips, already pale from the nearness of death.

"I told my Mary how much I loved her," he said to Mildred.

"And did Mary say anything to you, Walter?"

"Yes. Mary said, 'I've given you a daughter, my darling,' and she asked me to promise to love our daughter with all my heart."

Walter paused. He watched some children building a sandcastle until the lump left his throat and he could say, "We named our daughter Amy."

"Amy is a nice name, Walter."

Then Walter told about Amy growing into a young woman who was a willow in the wind, chilled cider on a hot day—a rainbow in the summer sky. "Amy was as pretty as a wildflower. Her hair fell to her shoulders like nightfall. Her eyes sparkled like diamonds in the moonlight."

Walter thought a moment, his leathered face polished with pride. "Amy was smart, too. She enrolled at State University, a good school not far from where we sit this very minute. Amy was to graduate in 1924.

"I had gone to visit her, and the two of us strolled from her dorm to the beach, and we were walking barefoot in the sand when I asked what Amy wanted for a graduation present."

"Did Amy say what she wanted?"

"She did, Mildred. She looked at me with eyes chock full of happiness, and she said to me, 'Pops, the one thing I want more than anything else is Ruby,' but that didn't make any sense to me at all."

"So what did you do, Walter?"

"Why, I thought about it a minute, and then I asked, 'What's Ruby, pumpkin?' and Amy smiled and took my hand, and we walked barefoot right up Main Street to a showroom window so clean and bright, you could see the sea and the clouds reflecting on the glass like a painting."

"And what about Ruby?"

"Why, Ruby was right there, Mildred. Displayed behind that window." His voice faded like a phonograph running down.

Mildred touched Walter's frail hands to remind him that he was telling a story. "What was Ruby, Walter?"

"Ruby was a Studebaker, Mildred. A 1924 Studebaker, Special 6 Tourister, mud flaps, cloth top."

"Red?"

"Red like a ruby. What a car! Running boards wide enough to haul pianos on. Spare tires set into the front fenders. Collapsible bumpers. A hood as long as a locomotive's. Chrome gleaming like glass. An overhanging boot. I sure understood why Amy wanted Ruby."

"What happened then, Walter?" The story had come to the part Mildred liked best. She did not want it to end.

"I said to Amy, 'Peaches, I will buy you Ruby on one condition. After your graduation, the two of us will take a trip. Let's drive down the coast, all the way to Mexico.' Amy hugged me and kissed me, and she asked, 'Pops, can we stop in Hollywood?' And I said, 'We will, peaches. Maybe Carmel, too.' I was so happy, I cried."

"How about San Francisco, Walter? Amy would have

liked the cable cars."

"San Francisco would have been nice. Anyway, I bought Ruby. I made the manager promise to hold her in storage until graduation day. He said he'd have the car ready with a big bow tied on her hood ornament. Amy could come pick her up whenever I said."

"Did she?"

Walter shook his head, blinking. The sun glistened against a tear trailing down his cheek.

"No. Amy took sick, Mildred. Polio. I tried everything. The best doctors. The latest medications. It was no use. I held a damp cloth trying to cool her fever when Amy smiled at me and whispered, 'I love you, Pops,' and then she closed her eyes and flew away to be with the angels."

"What happened to Ruby?" Mildred asked, very gently.

Walter shook his head. "I don't know. I never went back for Ruby. I couldn't. They sent me a couple of notices. I didn't respond."

The story usually ended there, just as the setting sun was coloring the clouds pink, and Mildred was comforting Walter, holding his hands.

But this day was different, as different as shadows at night or the stars at noon or flower gardens growing on the moon. On this day, Mildred took Walter's hands in hers and looked deep into his eyes—deep into his soul. She said, "I found Ruby, Walter."

No flicker of emotion crossed Walter's face. Only a slight quickening of his breath showed he had heard.

Mildred repeated herself. "I found Ruby, Walter. Will you come with me?"

For a long while, Walter couldn't answer. Then, shoulders stooped by the long years of heavy burden straightened. His weary hands unlaced themselves. His head lifted proudly. His eyes brightened. "Yes, Mildred. Yes!"

The next morning, Mildred and Walter walked Broadway to the old Studebaker building. The demolition gang assembled to raze the structure had not yet begun work. The foremen and his crew stood outside, gathered about a dusty, antiquated car. They sipped coffee from paper cups, waiting.

Walter approached, Mildred a step behind him. He reached out in disbelief to touch the car, the mirrors, the wilted bow tied to the hood ornament. He caressed grime from the car's hood. He caught his breath when he saw the exposed enamel—dusty, yet red. Deep red. Proud red. The red of apples in an autumn orchard.

The foreman crumpled his cup and tossed it away. He spat and removed his hard hat to wipe a sleeve across his mouth. "We pulled it from the basement yesterday, just as this lady came passing by," he said.

"I was on my way shopping," Mildred proudly said to Walter.

The foreman replaced his hard hat. "Found it buried in a pile of debris—1923 model. That makes her pretty damned old, but still brand new. Odometer shows nineteen miles. We're waiting for the building owner with word what to do."

Walter nodded slowly, in a trance. He opened the driver's door to touch the mohair, the wooden steering wheel and paneling, the chrome gadgets.

A moment later, the building owner arrived. "Took a while to check, but this car was purchased in 1924 by a Walter Robertson for his daughter. Both names were on the title, but neither ever claimed the vehicle. The dealer said he remembered the postman coming here trying to deliver a letter addressed to Walter Robertson. He placed that letter in the glove box along with the title. After a couple of months went by, he had the car stored in a corner of the basement." Then the owner glanced at Walter and asked, "You Robertson, Mister?"

"Yes."

"Well, I guess the Studebaker is yours. Say, check the glove box. See if that letter and the title are still there."

Walter mumbled something that could not be

understood. He reached for the latch slowly, reluctantly, and removed the title. Then he brought out a yellowed envelope with all the care of an archaeologist raising a scroll from its ancient hiding place. He unfolded a note penned on pink paper.

Dear Pops,

I am sitting up in my hospital bed so I can see out the window to the sea. There are sailboats flitting about, and my favorite kind of popcorn clouds everywhere, and I know I am going to die.

I love you, Pops. But I know how much you love me, too, and that frightens me more than dying ever could.

Since you lost Mother, you've loved no one except me. Not even yourself, I think. Death is faster and more final for the dying than for the living, as the living must endure death long after its happening.

So, Pops, be sad for me. Grieve for me, certainly. A day, a week perhaps, even a month if you must. Then find some wonderful person you want to share our love with, and who will love us in return.

Do it, Pops! Then the two of you take Ruby south toward Mexico. Remember how much I wanted to visit Hollywood? Well, when you stop at Hollywood, throw me a kiss on the wind, and know how very much I miss you.

Your loving daughter, Amy

Tears spattered the note like spring rain. Walter leaned against the old car for a moment, face buried in the crook of his arm. Then he wiped his nose on his sleeve, dried his eyes, and smiled at Mildred. "You think an old car like this could be fixed up?"

"Why, I would think so, Walter. They do wonders with old cars these days. And Ruby is a brand new, old car."

Walter folded the note into its envelope. He looked Ruby over then studied the clouds drifting overhead. "Mildred, let's say Ruby can be made to run. Let's say we get her all polished up and proud. Would you mind an old man asking you to go on a trip?"

"Depends on the old man, Walter."

"Let's say it was me."

"Might be interesting."

"South down the Coastal Highway?"

"They say the coast route is real pretty."

"Clear to Mexico with a stop in San Francisco?"

"Seeing the cable cars would be nice."

"And Hollywood?"

Mildred gave Walter a smile that soared like seagulls. "I would like that, Walter Robertson. I would like that very much."

"So, what does Kilimanjaro feel like?"

My Trek Through Tanzania

Rick Andriesian

Africa! What a place. What a concept. Imagine the biggest part of an 11,000,000 square mile continent that still has animals routinely maiming, killing, and eating people... Now *that's* a wild thought.

It was March 1986, and my friend Teri and I had set out to spend seventeen days in East Africa. I left with just a small pack, my passport, some cash, and a ticket to Arusha, Tanzania.

Being an independent type, I had no tour or hotel reservations, and only a vague plan to see some African animals and to climb Mt. Kilimanjaro. I had travelled quite a bit and had learned how to travel light, independently, and cheaply.

Travelling light is both an art and a science. From reading and from talking to fellow backpackers from dozens of countries, I've learned that as little as two changes of clothing in a knapsack are enough for some destinations. Add a sweater, raincoat, small tent, and a sleeping bag, and you can travel to almost any place carrying less than thirty pounds on your back.

By making your plans and arrangements as you go, you can travel independently at your own pace, and, if you just "wing it," at much less expense. You may not have the security or organization, or actually know the cost ahead of time, as when travelling with a tour group—which has a high cost. But with flexibility, a spirit of adventure, and an openness to whatever comes your way, you can have a much more interesting, satisfying, and unique trip.

Travelling cheaply is mostly a matter of discipline and practice. I learned I could eat well and sleep in a clean bed most anywhere in Africa, South America, and Asia for $200 to $400 per month—back in the 1980s. By being frugal and independent—and while maintaining a certain level of cleanliness—I planned to see much more of the world for not very much money. Included in my '80s adventures was my time in Tanzania.

While neighboring Kenya had excellent tourist facilities and was well known for its animals and parks, almost everything in socialist Tanzania was expensive and in short supply. The country was relatively underdeveloped and had an even higher concentration of game animals.

It was quite sobering to begin exploring the grounds of your hotel and find a sign that read:

DO NOT WALK BEYOND THE GARDEN AREA— VIOLATORS WILL BE EATEN.

You had better believe it. Not long before our arrival, one of the waiters missed the bus back to his village and was killed by a rhino as he walked the four miles home.

Once we'd checked in to our hotel, Teri and I wasted no time in making preparations for our days in Tanzania. Just hours after our arrival, she and I agreed on a plan, hired a Land Rover and driver, bought some black market gasoline, and set out.

Across the plains of East Africa we went with our driver, Mr. Goodluck, at the wheel. At Lake Manyara National Park, we were serenaded by trumpeting elephants that night. In the morning, we looked from our balcony, 300 feet straight down the cliff on which we were perched, and saw small groups of elephants wandering through the clearings below. Later, when we drove through the park, we observed giraffes, zebras, various antelope species, wildebeest, wart hogs, Cape buffalo, and hundreds of baboons, all up close. Seen from a distance, what we thought were rocks in the river turned into herds of hippos, bellowing and bawling loudly.

We left Lake Manyara and moved on across the plains. In the hill region, lush green farms were all too often striped by severely eroded streams, exposing deep gouges in the brick-red earth. Eventually, we reached a crest and saw one of the most impressive sights I've yet seen, the Ngorongoro Crater, the world's largest volcanic caldera.

Inside the Ngorongoro Conservation Area, the crater rises out of the forest on one side and has the famed Serengeti Plains on the other. It is ten to twelve miles across—three times the size of Oregon's Crater Lake National Park—and 2,000 feet deep, from the rim to the base of the caldera. Its floor covers over 100 square miles. Because of the year-round water supply—Lake Magadi is near its center, fed by natural springs and streams—most migratory animals stay all year. Consequently, they say it has the highest concentration of African game anywhere.

We were lucky to be there during the rainy season. While the rain kept most of the tourists away, it suited me just fine. The rain came several times each day, but it never lasted more than thirty minutes and made everything greener, cooler—although still in the eighties—and provided a dramatic and ever-changing horizon. Mr. Goodluck drove us around the rim and then down the muddy track to the crater floor.

We spent a full day cruising the tracks and roads through grasslands and groves of trees, and around shallow lakes. We saw dozens of lions from as close up as five feet. They appeared well fed, but we kept the windows up and the sunroof closed anyway. Flamingos, hartebeest, waterbucks, dik-dik, zebras, and others animals were caught by our cameras. We also got within thirty to forty feet of two very rare white rhinos. That was scarier than being five feet from a lion. Just watching these beasts for ten to fifteen minutes in the wild was worth the trip.

It may not be long before we don't have a chance to see a rhino because "rhino wars" continue in Africa—rangers versus poachers. The rangers have a new policy: SHOOT TO KILL anyone seen carrying a gun in a national park. But, even with this policy, the rhino population is still dropping toward extinction.

We stopped for a picnic lunch in a beautiful grove of trees by the lake. Although the only animals we had seen for two to three miles were acres of zebras, in Africa, you don't know what is watching you from the tall grass. When it was time to use the outhouse, our guide said not to worry.

But imagine walking from your picnic table to the outhouse 100 feet away and not being sure you would come back alive. That's how it felt. We were watching all sides for snakes, lions, etc. We did make it there and back without trouble—only to have kite problems during lunch.

Kites are medium-sized, falcon-type birds—one of over 500 bird species found in the area. Honestly, during our lunch stop, it was like a scene from Alfred Hitchcock's 1963 film, *The Birds*. As we sat at the base of a tree to eat, we noticed first one, then several kites circling overhead. They landed just above us and were eyeing us greedily from twenty feet up in the branches. Suddenly, there was a swoop of wings as one tried to take the food from my hand. Gradually, about fifteen birds were perched all around and over us at a distance of only ten to twenty feet, watching for their chance for free food from an inattentive tourist.

We were dive-bombed maybe twenty times in twenty minutes. It was *not* a relaxing lunch. They never got any food, nor did they touch us, but we could have hit them easily had we not merely been trying to shoo them away. I guess that's what you call "adventures in dining."

Even a bigger thrill than the lions, rhinos, and kites was the spotting of cheetahs at the end of the day. For half an hour, we followed a pair of these seldom-seen cats who couldn't seem to decide if they were hungry or not. They were lying in the grass when we spotted them, and we approached in the Land Rover to about 100 feet.

Suddenly, they spotted a nearby antelope, got up, and froze with ears flattened back. You could see them listening, tensing their muscles, and could sense them calculating the distance, angles, and speed necessary to bring down their prey. The cheetahs took a few steps forward and seemed ready to spring, when first one, then the other, literally flopped down in the grass as if to say, "Aw, to heck with it. Let's just go out for a pizza later."

After five minutes of dozing and grooming, they got up again as they sensed a hartebeest. This process was repeated three or four times, each with a different potential prey. Each time, we expected to see "the drama of life and death in Africa." Each time they flopped down, and we started laughing. It was hysterical. They never did attack or chase anything while we watched. It was as if the Cheetah Comedy Troupe was performing a *Saturday Night Live* skit for our amusement.

Our other major destination was Mt. Kilimanjaro National Park, located just south of the equator on the Kenya-Tanzania border. At 19,340 feet, volcanic, glacier-topped Mt. Kilimanjaro is Africa's highest peak. It is a very challenging trek. No ropes are required, but it is extremely taxing as you climb almost three vertical miles on the twenty-two mile hike up the slope.

Teri and I spent two nights relaxing and acclimatizing to the 5,000-foot elevation at a hotel near the park entrance. Then we hired a guide and four porters, and set off. We started along a broad path through the tropical rain forest. Since we were in unfamiliar territory, we asked our guide, David, about local hazards.

He said, "Except for the green mamba snake and the occasional leopard higher up, there's nothing to worry about."

That reassurance didn't exactly make for carefree hiking. I've had dozens of encounters with black bears, rattlesnakes, and scorpions in the western United States, and I'm respectful, but not nervous. I've never hiked in grizzly bear country in the United States—even the thought of it makes me nervous—but I could do it.

However, animals whose behavior I'm not familiar with, and predators going out of their way to attack or eat people, make me really nervous. With a fair amount of foot traffic on the trail, it wasn't likely we would see any snakes, but we watched our step very closely that first day. As it turned out, the only wildlife we saw were troops of monkeys. Whew!

The rainforest gradually thinned out near the end of the first day. The Madara Hut where we camped was in a clearing above 9,000 feet. The Park Service had put up small eight-bunk A-frame shelters and provided mattresses. There was also a cookhouse, an A-frame dining hall, an outhouse, and cold water on tap—very civilized.

We chatted with some Japanese trekkers, ate our dinner, and watched the afternoon shadows lengthen across the African plain over a mile below us. It was impressive to watch the thunderclouds build below at sunset, and to look *down* at the flashes of lightening as night fell. What a view!

During the night, Teri and I heard occasional rain on the roof, also the screams and howls of monkeys in the trees and on our doorstep. It was fun, spooky, and exciting. We kept the door to the hut locked.

An hour into our second day's hike, we rose above the forest and entered the Alpine Moorland Zone. Initially, the moorland is lush with tall grass, bushes, and occasional groves of small trees. But, as you climb higher, the temperature gets cooler, precipitation decreases, and the vegetation gets shorter and sparser. Even a ten-minute walk farther up the trail was enough to notice small changes—it was remarkable and dramatic. And, of course, with every step, Kilimanjaro came more sharply into focus.

Toward the end of the second day, we entered a narrow belt encircling the mountain, where the climatic conditions are just right for the giant groundsel plant. This is the strangest looking plant I have ever seen—hard to describe. It's roughly the shape of a ten- to twenty-foot tall cactus, except its trunk and "arms" have hairy leaves. It looks like it would be right at home on Mars. In fact, as a child, I once saw a science fiction movie in which the space monsters all looked just like this plant. It was all remarkably eerie and otherworldly.

We had been hiking under cloudy skies most of the day, but as we arrived at the Horombo Hut Camp at 12,300 feet, the sun broke through. We were cool, tired, dirty, and short of breath, so the warmth, the brilliant light, and the stunning view of the plains 8,000 to 9,000 thousand feet below perked us up.

Our guides brought us hot tea and a delicious meal, and this was followed by a bucket of hot water—the Third World's famous bucket bath. It's amazing that you can learn to do a shampoo and nearly a full bath with one gallon of water. It was the perfect end to an exciting day.

Most trekkers go up Kilimanjaro in three and a half days, and down in one and a half, but Teri and I had arranged an extra day and two nights at Horombo to rest and acclimatize. After waving goodbye to our fellow trekkers on their way up the mountain, we had the camp to ourselves. We *rested* by taking a four-hour hike to the base of Mawenzi (Kilimanjaro's twin peak at 16,890 feet). The highlight of this day's hike was cloud watching and "cloud walking."

Over several hours, we watched as clouds formed over the hot plains below. Soon, armies of thick clouds raced up the mountain forced by rising hot air. Some passed a few feet overhead. Other more wispy clouds rolled along the ground and up the slope. Still others had such a solid appearance as they rose toward us at twenty miles per hour, it seemed like we would be knocked over by them. We weren't, but when we couldn't see our feet because of the thick clouds surrounding them, it did seem like we were flying or cloud walking.

After our second night at Horombo Hut, we pressed onward to our final camp at the base of the cone. On this, our fourth day, we were in the alpine desert zone. Early in the day's hike, our porter gathered the last dead twigs for that night's cook fire. Another porter filled a five-gallon jug at the last spring, and for six miles, balanced it on his head.

The climatic conditions gradually became so harsh that we left behind the last bush, insect, and lizard. Moss, lichens, and small, low clumps of pale grass were all that grew on the dry and rocky ground. Now it was only us, the mountain, and the gray clouds overhead.

The day was cool and windy, but we were dressed for it. The trail was good, and most of the time had only a mild incline. While we had long since left the lush rainforest and giant groundsel, the desolate beauty of the slope, the gray clouds racing overhead, and the peak itself looming before us, gave us plenty to look at. But, the effects of altitude made themselves known with every step.

Mild nausea and headaches didn't bother Teri and me as much as it did some others, but the shortness of breath slowed my friend and me to a snail's pace. With the hut in sight, we took one-and-a-half hours to walk the final mile. Our pace was walk, then stagger a hundred yards, sit a minute, then stagger seventy yards, sit to catch our breath for several minutes, then stagger another forty yards, and rest even longer. We were breathing hard, gasping from the lack of oxygen. It seemed, at times, we'd never make it—but we did!

Kibo Hut, sitting at 15,500 feet, was a four-room stone dormitory with forty bunks and a cookhouse. Our previous four days had been just a warm up. The main event started just outside our door.

There, Kilimanjaro's main cone erupted steeply out

of the mountain's relatively gentle flanks. Our guides fed us early, sang us a few songs, and put us to bed at six in the evening. Just after midnight, we were awakened and given hot tea and sugar cookies for breakfast. By 1:00 a.m. in the morning, we were warmly dressed and on the trail, intending to reach the top before sunrise.

The previous day's inspection of our route showed it to be a zigzag trail up a thirty- to fifty-degree slope of loose rock. It was a 3,500 foot vertical climb, and if all our steps were laid end-to-end, they would total less than one-and-a-half miles. For this trek, our guides had allowed five hours. But, while climbing by lantern and flashlight in the twenty-eight degree cold, and gasping for breath with every step, it didn't seem to Teri and me like nearly enough time.

I'll confess now: I didn't make the summit. Approximately fifty-percent of climbers do make it to the summit—but only one out of five people attempting that day reached it. At age thirty-three, I was very lean, fit, and in the best shape of my life.

By 3:30 a.m. in the morning, we had huffed and puffed our way to the halfway mark—just over 17,000 feet. By this point, I was reduced to a single step, then a need to rest more than a minute. Every step I took, I nearly fainted. Teri was doing better than I.

For me, the combination of frozen feet, nausea, gasping for each breath, and severe faintness made me decide to turn back. It was amazing that what took me two-and-a-half hours to climb, I descended in about twenty minutes. Teri and her guide continued on.

I was breathing much easier but was severely disappointed when I returned to the hut. Luckily, I had a Plan B. I pulled out the telescope and tripod I had carried with me all over Africa.

Halley's Comet orbits the earth and deep space once every seventy-six years and is visible for only a few weeks. I had hoped to view the comet from the top of Kilimanjaro, but through the high altitude, clear equatorial skies at Kibo Hut, the view of the comet was just fine. In this otherworldly place, I had an out-of-this-world view.

Teri returned at 5:30 a.m. in the morning. She and her guide had continued another one-and-a-half hours to 18,000 feet before turning back. We viewed the comet for a while, napped until 10:00 a.m., and then headed down the mountain. In addition to our climb in the dark, we walked about fifteen to seventeen miles down to the Mandara Hut at 9,000 feet. It made for a long, hard day.

High-altitude mountain sickness kills people from lack of air pressure and oxygen. The park rangers don't have money for a helicopter for the rapid descent required to save the life of persons affected by this. But, they do have strong legs and a stout metal stretcher with a single motorcycle wheel under the frame. We saw this contraption at Kibo Hut, and another man we met saw it in use several days earlier.

Imagine the sinking feeling in your gut if you were just starting up the mountain and saw two exhausted-looking rangers who were on the last mile of a fifteen- to twenty-mile run downhill with a loaded stretcher. The rangers are credited with numerous lives saved each year. They are dedicated and hard working.

In most places I travel to, I like to make time to just sit and open my senses to what is around me. Whether it is a cultural scene like a village market, man-made wonder like the pyramids, or on one of nature's grandest mountains, I like to go beyond the five basic human senses. I try to open my mind and spirit to soak up the feelings of a place—like the cliché, "picking up vibes."

So, what does Kilimanjaro feel like? I could almost feel it rippling its muscles. It gave me the feeling of being exposed, like I was a flea on an elephant's back. Opening myself to experiences like that helps me keep life in perspective. As with most places I've been, I'd like to return.

As much as I enjoy the different cultures and natural wonders of the places I visit, it's meeting the people along the way that's the most enjoyable. Our driver, Mr.

Goodluck, our guide, David, and our porters, Humphrey and Richard, were all very good to us and great company, as well.

Our Australian friend, Heather, was very interesting to talk to. She was travelling solo in Europe and Africa for a year. She appeared to be of average build and fitness but was the only one of five trekkers to make it to the top of Kilimanjaro that day. We also met a priest from Uganda at the airport. He gave us a fascinating overview of Ugandan history while we waited for our flight home. He was supervisor of missions for six East African countries.

While gassing up our vehicle, we met a seventeen-year-old soldier girl who struck up a conversation with us. I played with six village kids, ages five to eleven, in a creek-side pool. We met a young man named John, who walked us through the forest near the hotel at the base of Mt. Kilimanjaro, and a young wheat farmer from Corvallis, Oregon—a city only eighty miles from my home—while half-way around the world. What a small world it is! All of these, and dozens of brief encounters with other people, really made the trip memorable.

I have particularly fond memories of Jonathon, a waiter at the Ngorongoro Hotel. Always polite, gentle, and wanting to talk, Jonathon invited us to his home on our next-to-last day in Tanzania. It was our loss we hadn't accepted his offer sooner. He, his wife, and his daughter, Potutee, lived in a relatively modern, government-built concrete apartment surrounded by forest. Although their apartment was a single, bunker-like room, Jonathon and his wife's graciousness and hospitality would have charmed the Queen of England. He was obviously pleased and proud we had visited his home and village.

Jonathon's friendliness and hospitality inspired me to be as welcoming and hospitable to foreigners visiting my hometown in the Pacific Northwest. Truly, world travel has made me a better man, and I look forward to my next international adventure.

Rick Andriesian is a life-long Oregonian. Growing up, he went to school in Cottage Grove, Warrenton, Astoria, and Portland. He graduated from Oregon Health Sciences University in 1976 with a BSN in Nursing and has worked for most of his forty-one years as an RN in ERs in Portland area hospitals.

As a whitewater rafter, Rick has made river trips throughout the western United States, Canada, Chile, the Philippines, Australia, New Zealand, and Pakistan. In 1988, he made a solo around-the-world bicycle tour. The thirteen-month trip included Nepal, India, Thailand, Australia, New Zealand, and northern Pakistan. Overall, Rick has visited forty countries on six continents.

Rick has two grown sons, and he has been married for over eleven years to Deni. They hope to travel extensively in the future.

"Darling, I thought
I'd never get through."

Overseas Calling

Jean Young

It was a hard time to be a military wife. World War II was raging, and my husband, Lieutenant Dale Young, was an Army pilot.

We were living on base in Texas at the time, and one afternoon, he came home and told me he'd been given new orders. He would be leaving soon for England.

Dale wrote me frequently while he was stationed near Cambridge, but he was eventually sent to France, and then Austria, near Vienna. His plane hauled parachutists and supplies.

I returned home to the Seattle, Washington, area while my husband was overseas. I went back to work at Boeing, and I felt useful and liked my co-workers. Sadly, mail from Europe was spotty and I was lonely, even living at home.

Near the war's end, Dale wrote about the prisoners they took from an Austrian prison to Greece. He said the men were skeletal, and the flyers gave them all the rations they had on the plane.

The food actually made the malnourished men sick. They didn't know what happened to the men after they delivered them and often wondered if they had even survived.

When the war was over, Seattle went crazy. Our office carpool drove in to the city, and we joined the crowds.

People filled the streets, shouting, singing, going nowhere, excited and thrilled.

Almost every store closed. We finally found an open restaurant and ate, and we headed home about midnight. My husband would be coming home soon!

Dale wrote that he had found out that calls to the U.S. could be made from Switzerland. He had applied for leave and was going skiing. He would call me from St. Moritz. He set the date for Saturday.

I was so excited. I called his mother, Nina, and suggested she come over and share the call. I felt very noble.

Saturday came. We waited. We waited, and waited. No call.

Nina went to bed about 10:00 p.m. I stayed up until 2:00 a.m. I couldn't sleep. What had happened?

On Sunday, Nina went home. No call.

I stayed home on Monday. No call. I went back to work Tuesday, dashing home the minute my shift was over. Nothing. And nothing on Wednesday, either.

There was a smallpox scare in Seattle, and on Thursday, I waited to get a vaccination before I went home.

When I got there, Mother shouted, "Where have you been? Your call is coming through!"

I couldn't believe it. Dale and I would really be able to talk—to hear each other. I waited.

The phone rang. I shook so hard, I could barely pick up the receiver. "Hello?"

"Your call from Zurich is coming through," the operator replied.

Zurich?

"There have been storms over the Atlantic causing delays," the operator continued. "I will stay on the line to assist you if necessary. Go ahead, Lieutenant."

"Darling, I thought I'd never get through."

"Oh. Oh, it seemed so long. I'm so thrilled. Your mother had to go home, but I'll call her and tell her."

"Mother?" His voice faded a bit.

"Yes, Mother."

The operator cut in. "Mother."

"Oh." He went on. "I got a present for you. A real Swiss watch."

"Why, how nice." But, I'd gotten a new watch for my birthday.

"And I got your picture. I loved it, though it made me miss you even more."

"Oh, good." It didn't sound like Dale. Could he have been drinking? And he'd written that he hadn't liked the picture I'd sent him. "Uh... you're in Zurich, not St. Moritz?"

"Yes, of course, though I've got to leave for Biarritz tomorrow. I'm so glad our call finally got through."

"Biarritz? When did you..." I paused.

The operator said, "Biarritz. Your time is up."

He said he loved me. I said I loved him, and I hung up.

He didn't sound like himself. I couldn't remember his voice... When had he left Vienna? Where was Biarritz?

Tears formed. Shaking, I went to my bedroom. A picture? A watch? My husband, a man whose voice I couldn't remember...

I lay on my bed and cried. I'd have to write him and say he should go to his parents' when he came home. We would have to meet, and then see what could be worked out.

I cried some more.

I was rousted from my misery when my mother called up the stairs, "Your call is coming through!"

A call? But, I'd had my call. I ran down and picked up the phone.

"I thought I'd never get through," a man said.

It was my husband's voice! He had been unable to book a call all week, due to the storms. He'd fallen asleep, waiting.

He said he had skied all week and loved it. We'd have to go skiing when he got back.

He loved me. He said he loved me!

The three-minute call was over so quickly. I

remembered my husband. He would come home to me soon.

I never found out who the man was I had talked to earlier. I hoped he, too, got his real call through.

Jean Young was born in Wenatchee, Washington, and lived most of her life in the Seattle area in the log home she and her husband built in the 1960s. A retired senior center director, Jean filled her days with volunteer work, reading, gardening, international travel, and spending time with her children, grandchildren, and great-grandchildren.

Mrs. Young wrote two published works, Midlife Senior Moments, *a fictional story about a widow who goes to work at a senior center, and* Charlie, the Dog Who Could Sing, *a children's chapter book.*

Jean passed away in September of 2016.

"I wrote a note to my grandparents
and a tearful letter to Hans."

Uprooted

Muschi Mayflower

I had never heard of Tennessee Williams, and my glass menagerie didn't include a unicorn, but it did have a giraffe that I especially liked and really wanted to take with me. Except, wouldn't they question me? Why would a seventeen-year-old take a glass giraffe to a doctor's appointment?

And then it dawned on me—how silly to dwell on such a small thing, considering that in a couple of days, I would have to leave *everything* behind, never to see it again. Even more importantly, all my friends, my grandparents, my dog, and our cat would no longer be part of my daily life. And here I was worrying about my glass animal collection.

I guess it was the suddenness of my family's decision to escape from East Germany that I found overwhelming. It was so hard to think clearly! Could I truly not tell my grandparents, my best friends, or even Hans, my very first true love? Of course, I knew the answer. Under the totalitarian East German regime, one could trust no one—fear, greed, and power seeking thrive in such conditions and lead to betrayal.

Worried about being expelled from high school, it had become second nature for me not to mention my true political opinions...although I had managed a protest of sorts by not joining the Free German Youth organization. Secretly, some of us entertained ourselves by labeling someone either a tomato or a radish, meaning tomato red—communist through and through, or radish red—only on the outside. But we usually didn't dare to put our guesses to the test.

And how shocked and sad my mother's parents would be! My brother and I were their only grandchildren. They had brought us up after their daughter escaped to West Germany a few years after the end of World War II. Like many others, she hoped to start a new and better life, away from the oppressive Russian occupation forces and the rest of communism.

When she said good-bye to my brother and me, she promised to send for us as soon as she was able to make a living. Our father had been a prisoner of war in Russia for years. He was alive, but no one knew if or when he might be one of the lucky fifteen percent who survived and actually made it back home.

Yet, about a year later when Dieter, my brother, was ten and I was seven, our grandma suddenly told us that we had to go to the railroad station to meet our father. He got off the train, looking for his wife, but found only his mother-in-law and two children. We all hugged him dutifully—even though he was a stranger. After all, he had been gone for seven years.

No doubt, while suffering all the horrors and deprivations of a Russian concentration camp, our dad had looked forward to seeing his family, as well as returning his shoe stores from their disastrous post-war state to their former glory. He had been one of the county's best known and respected merchants, so who would blame him for not wanting to start over penniless in the West.

Yet, as might be expected, our parents had become estranged. Our mother refused to come back to East Germany, and our father's love for her turned to hatred. Bad news—especially for us kids and our grandparents. No Golden West for us.

The East German courts gave custody to our father, who promptly asked his former parents-in-law to leave the house. He strictly limited our visits with them and forbade contact with our mother. Too bad the honeymoon with this new dad, who played with us at first and told us war stories, didn't last long. He turned out to be an embittered, angry, authoritarian man who ruled with an iron hand.

So here I was, ten years older, looking at my cute glass menagerie lined up on the shelf above my desk that I was to empty of anything too personal. My father and stepmother were feverishly going through everything and burning, burying, or otherwise destroying what they could before we were to leave—which would be in a couple of days. We couldn't help but picture our home being invaded by those hateful state and party functionaries who would surely snoop into everything and take what they wanted. Who would take care of my Spitz, Putzi, and all my plants?

Why did we have to leave so suddenly and urgently? Most of the professionals, merchants, tradesmen, and farmers had long since escaped to the West, usually not waiting until their possessions were expropriated. Yet Dad had hung in there. He just couldn't face leaving his beloved stores and home, hoping against hope that re-unification with the West would surely come one day soon.

Then a little more than a year before the Berlin Wall went up, he was tipped off by a well-connected friend. "Try to escape or be jailed for 'income tax evasion.'" This was a convenient, trumped-up charge leveled by the government against those few remaining business owners who were too successful and too much competition for the poorly run, state-owned stores. And it always led to seizure of property, plus imprisonment. Through guilt by association, our stepmother's bookstore and art gallery would likely be confiscated as well.

Those last two days were very sad and scary, and yet very exciting, even propitious for me. On the one hand, leaving behind so many people I cared about was almost more than I could bear. Plus, I was in the midst of final exams and wouldn't be able to graduate with my class of only twenty-eight seniors in a city of 45,000—and that really hurt.

Coming from a family of so-called capitalists, I'd had little chance of getting a higher education. It was only by special dispensation that I had made it into high school at all, for our government followed a policy of reverse discrimination by allowing only "working class" children a higher education. On the other hand, in West Germany, I would be able to choose my field of college study. Here in the East, someone like me would be restricted to agriculture or chemistry, the fields where professionals were currently needed.

I was beginning to like the idea of this new life we were going to lead. No more worrying about what I could safely say and whom I could trust, no more of those constant marches for socialism and against "American imperialism," no more standing in line for scarce or rationed food, no more hiding the fact that I occasionally went to church.

Instead, I would probably see some of my friends again who had left over the past few years. I would have access to whatever books I wished to read or television programs I wanted to watch, not just those published or originating on our side of the Iron Curtain. I could eat as many bananas and oranges as I wanted, listen to jazz and rock-n-roll—forbidden here as "too American"—get pretty clothes. The icing on the cake? I'd find a way to see my mother again, as soon as I could do it without my father's knowledge.

The night before we left, I wrote a note to my grandparents and a tearful letter to Hans, the boy with whom I was in love. I had to mail them before departing, because correspondence from West Germany was routinely opened and could endanger the recipient. By the time the letters arrived, we would be safely on the other side. Or would we?

I had pushed from my mind any thoughts of the very real danger of being arrested at the border in Berlin. At the time—before the Wall was erected—it was still possible to traverse the so-called French, British, or American sectors of Berlin by subway or train in order to get to one's destination in the Soviet Sector. That was our plan.

Berlin was situated in East Germany, and our city, Stendal, was only about an hour's drive from it. At the checkpoint, we would have to show our IDs and hope that we were not on the authorities' list of potential fugitives from the German Democratic Republic. Of course, we would split up rather than board as a group. Moreover, we prepared ourselves for questioning by each having a story at the ready about our reasons for wanting to spend a few hours in the Soviet Sector, on the opposite side of Berlin from where we had to set out.

I don't know how all eight of us piled into my father's twenty-five-year-old Ford V8 at dawn that day. Along with our parents—and by then, four kids—our little group included the store's accountant and my stepmother's maiden aunt. We all watched the roads with trepidation, for fear that someone would notice and blow the whistle on us. Theoretically, no one would know that we had left until my father and stepmother didn't arrive to open the stores on Monday morning.

In Potsdam, on the outskirts of Berlin, my dad sadly parked the car and got on a subway train. The car was his pride and joy. It had been kept hidden during the war and was one of few automobiles in our town. Actually, by that time, you could purchase a car manufactured in an Eastern-Bloc country—as long as the ten-year waiting period didn't bother you.

Our stepmother, with six-year-old Christian and three-year-old Gundula in tow, took the next train, and then each of us followed on separate ones. The trick was to be nonchalant—while my heart was beating like crazy—when the train stopped at the border crossing. I was wearing my best Sunday clothes but carried only a tiny purse. Watching as the police boarded the train, I hoped, *Please let me be questioned by a female who might understand that I supposedly need to see a dermatology specialist for my teenage acne.*

That part went well, but then I had to worry about the fate of the others. We had agreed to meet at the zoo in the British Sector. However, if one of us had been held at the checkpoint as a possible escapee and didn't show up, the rest of us would go back to Stendal as if nothing had happened. That way, there would be no proof that we had tried to leave, and whoever had been arrested would probably not be held for very long.

It was common practice to arrest fugitives' relatives and put them under extreme pressure in order to force their family's return to the East. The loss of almost three million productive citizens had become an enormous problem for the German Democratic Republic, a fact that a little later prompted the erection of the Berlin Wall.

The first stop in the Golden West was a revelation. The colors, the lights, no war ruins or run-down buildings in sight, people in fashionable clothes, vendors selling tropical fruit, Coca Cola, chewing gum—I longed to buy some of it, but my East German money was no good there. The cash we had dared to take with us could be exchanged, but it was worth only twenty-five percent of its value, so money would be very scarce.

Finally, the train stopped at the zoo station. I made my way to the zoo entrance and was relieved to find most of the others there already. But where was our father? Had he been detained because his name was on that dreaded list? The next few minutes were torture.

When at last he walked up, somewhat sheepishly, I had never been so glad to see him as I was at that moment! He had simply gotten off one stop too soon.

We didn't get to see the animals that day because we had to apply for asylum at the refugee camp before evening. I thought the camp was an amazing place—like something out of a novel. We were assigned to bunk beds in barren rooms, were issued a tin cup and soup bowl, and waited in long lines at mealtimes. But we were free!—with lots of time for dreaming of what life would be like once an American plane had flown us west to the Federal Republic of Germany, and lots of time for thinking of all we had left behind.

And the glass giraffe? It didn't get to go with me to the other side that day, but the tiniest of black glass cats did. And so did my teddy bear, Hansi, a parting gift from my mother before she left for the West ten years earlier.

My parents had allowed me to include one item in a "gift package" we mailed to friends in West Germany on that last day before our escape, and I had chosen Hansi. He and the kitty accompanied me in all my wanderings to the six countries, many states, and many, many cities where I lived before I settled in Astoria, Oregon. And they are with me still!

World War II was the cause of the events I have recalled and was started by Germany. As I have written them down today, on this sixtieth anniversary of Germany's surrender, May 8, 2005, I am saddened that wars are still very much a part of our lives. Yet, I am also happy to say, that in the forty years I have spent in this nation, I have always felt welcomed, despite my having been born in a former enemy country.

I feel at home in the United States, have seen quite a bit of it, and have brought up two sons here. Apart from my occupation as a visual artist, I have worked in a variety of interesting jobs, including translating four languages. Since 1993, I have been happily settled in Astoria.

Muschi Mayflower

"The Cherokee in him gave Daddy a strong incentive to live off the land and to respect it."

Another Wham Brake Story

Mary Ann Ylipelto

Why my dad was continually drawn to the God-forsaken swamp is still a mystery to me. It is definitely a man thing. Wham Brake was in northeastern Louisiana outside of Monroe somewhere. The bird hunting and fishing were equally dependable there. It was my Daddy's favorite haunt.

After one of his trips, Daddy came home with a knot the size of a plum on his right shin, which caused him various medical problems for over a year. While running—I use the term loosely here—the kind of running you do where the surf meets the sea, or in a vat of maple syrup, smack! Daddy came in contact with a log just underwater at shin level. He came home limping badly. You get the picture. I don't think it was possible to come home from the Wham in one piece.

On another trip, my Uncle Rob from Fort Worth went along for the fun. The particular part of the Wham into which they ventured was near a well site and consisted of an old oxbow lake that was good for white perch fishing. They shared a minnow bucket, and my dad had a stringer on his belt. They had waded out a ways, leaving their supplies in a duck blind, or on some high spot. My dad had caught several fish and hooked them on his stringer. All of a sudden, a water moccasin appeared and began snapping at the fish.

These snakes swim and raise their heads up out of the water, cobra style, and hiss at you with stinky breath while exposing a mouthful of sharp teeth. And this guy was over six feet long. The dictionary refers to the species as, "a venomous pit viper kin to a copperhead." Lovely, huh?

So there was my dad, only able to beat at the snake with his fishing rod as he moved toward a large log. As the snake continued its advance, my uncle ran to get their gun, moving so fast he might've walked on water! Daddy abandoned his fishing rod in favor of a stick that he broke off the log and was using it to beat at the snake.

To keep his balance, he used his left arm to grab the stump of the large branch sticking out of the log. Just about that time, Rob came back with their gun and was able to shoot the water moccasin. But then, the rotting stump that Daddy was holding gave way—and out flew a whole hive of guinea wasps! They stung him all over his face, neck, and hands. When he came home, he looked like he had the chicken pox—but he was happy!

Mother and I got to the point where we were torn between the fear of losing Daddy entirely to the swamp or looking forward with anticipation to the next great story he'd bring home. Also, even though Mother and I did more than enough cleaning and plucking, we always had plenty of fresh fish—mostly bass, bream, white perch, or catfish. Fried crisp and dredged in cornmeal, we practically lived off those four types of fish, along with the fowl Daddy shot, and an occasional deer.

The Cherokee in him gave Daddy a strong incentive to live off the land and to respect it.

As he grew older, he was fond of saying, "I used to be the best bass fisherman in the world, and the older I get, the better I get!"

Although an only child with no descendants, Mary Ann Ylipelto can't resist setting down all the wonderful stories from her childhood.

"We discovered some *friendly* skunks swiping our meat supply."

Daphne Grove

Wanda Hoffman Labart

"Hey! Let's go camping!"

After much discussion, and even more planning, we six neighborhood teenage girls—who lived mostly east of Myrtle Point, Oregon, around the Hoffman Bridge and before Broadbent—along with one very brave and unsuspecting mother, set out for Daphne Grove on the South Fork of the Coquille River. All our camping gear was stowed on the flatbed of the old farm truck of Melva and Lucille's parents, who dropped us off and left us on our own for four days and nights.

Setting up the tent was a real challenge, especially since we discovered it had been used as a tent house over a floor with walls extending up each side for about three feet. Our problem was, it was a borrowed tent. We couldn't cut the poles and lower it to ground level—no saw anyway—so it gave us no privacy at all. Thank goodness we were the only campers in the campground.

A good swim afterwards was fun, except brrrrrrr, that water was cold! But, we had our first experience skinny-dipping. Remember—no other campers. We did constantly check, though.

After supper and clean up, which was rinsing the dishes in the creek, scrubbing them with sand, and giving them a final rinse with hot water from the old blackened tea kettle, it was time to think about settling in for the night.

Since the tent was no protection, we each picked a spot to spread out our bedroll. There weren't sleeping bags back then—at least we didn't have any. Come to think of it, it was my first camping trip, and none of us had any of the now "necessary" gear.

After much changing of spots—rocks and sticks aren't very comfortable to sleep on—we finally settled down for the night. Or so we thought.

What was that noise?

Upon investigation, we discovered some *friendly* skunks swiping our meat supply. With the aid of our flashlight, we managed to hang what was left of the food from the trees, and with all the noise we made, the skunks disappeared. Fortunately for us, they left no calling cards.

We all had somewhat old-fashioned names: Alma, Wanda, Melva, Lucille, Louise, and Patricia. Remember, we were born in the 1920s. But all of us had nicknames too: Flower, Sunny, Junior, Shorty, Toughie, and Bumps—in honor of the mosquitoes, which just about ate us alive.

One vivid memory for me was when we were sitting at the plank table eating lunch. Toughie kept staring at me and suddenly reached across the table and slapped my face. She claimed she was after a mosquito. Oh, sure! I just about got mad enough to slap her back—but then, I just started laughing.

One evening during the trip, we were building sandcastles down by the creek and we heard a scream. We finally got everyone quiet—then we heard it again, several times. We decided it had to be a car wreck up the road beyond the campground. Someone was injured and needed help.

We hurriedly gathered some equipment—the axe, shovel, flashlight, and the first aid kit. Mom took the twenty-two rifle we had with us—it had been a present from her husband when they were first married to protect her chickens from hawks. We all walked quickly up the road looking for the person in trouble.

Flower, who wasn't really in favor of our trek, kept complaining about our wild-goose-chasing after a cougar. As it turned out, it could very well have been what we were doing—since after walking a good distance, no sign of any accident was found. No one slept too well that night.

Sunday, we hiked to China Flats. It was such a hot, hot day! The walk seemed miles farther than it actually was, but we were rewarded with company, and they had brought food—and was it ever good! After our episode with the skunks, our food supply was limited. We weren't going to starve, but boy, that fried chicken and chocolate cake was GREAT! It was sure nice of Pat's Aunt Jean and Uncle Duke to meet us there with goodies.

There was lots of singing around our campfires in the evenings, and just a great time being a group of girlfriends out camping together. Even Mom enjoyed it. But, it must have been a worrisome time for her with six girls to be responsible for. She was a courageous lady.

Finally, the day arrived when our truck returned to pick us up and take us home. What a wonderful time we had at Bare Skin Camp. Even after more than sixty years, the memories are still sweet.

"I can see the big E—
and the two Es below!"

Good Work Is Satisfying

Carl Abraham

Sometime in the mid '50s, at the beginning of the Cold War, while Dwight D. Eisenhower was still president, I saw him on TV wearing the glasses I had renovated for him about a year before. He was in the White House, and I was in St. Louis where all the glasses for the military came through our shop—the U.S. Army Medical and Therapy Unit.

Although there were 300 of us technicians, this particular prescription, to be inserted into the accompanying older Army-issued, silver-plated nickel frames, came to my desk. I read his name on the order, did the actual work of grinding the lenses and beveling them to fit. He probably had another dozen back-ups, but without at least one of them, he wouldn't have been able to read.

President Eisenhower's glasses were certainly the most famous I ever worked on. But, it was an additional twenty-five years, and after my retirement, before I began my most satisfying work with the Lions Club Sight and Hearing Charity.

During this time, I made many Mercy Ship trips— first to Jamaica, then many other countries: El Salvador, Honduras, Mexico, Nicaragua, Poland, Ukraine, and West Samoa. But the trip I remember best was to the land-locked country of El Salvador.

We went there by ship but rode in the back of uncovered pickups about 100 miles inland to La Union. It usually didn't rain there, except for about fifteen minutes around 2:00 p.m. in the afternoon, and we were out and under cover by then.

One particular time, it didn't matter if it rained or not, because I missed the last call to board the convoy of pickups and had to take a taxi the 100 miles—which cost me $100 out-of-pocket. I would've hated to miss the trip, however, because the following incident was so memorable.

Late in the afternoon, an ordinary looking, about thirty-five-year-old woman with a baby girl in her arms, stepped up in line. She sat down in my chair. I adjusted the Retromax, and within seconds, the machine informed me her prescription was minus sixteen—which meant she couldn't see past three inches.

The pickup trucks, each carrying their half a dozen technicians—of which I had not been one that day—had also dutifully pulled covered trailers containing 15,000 or 16,000 pair of Lions Club used-and-discarded glasses donated by Americans. These had all been numbered and boxed in order.

I went to search for as close a match to this frightfully short-distanced reading prescription as I could find. I found a minus fourteen and brought it to her. The frame fit fairly well. I only had to adjust them a bit around the ears.

I asked her if she could see the big E on the chart. She said she couldn't. She had never seen anything that far away—about ten feet. She seemed terrified, and her brain evidently needed time to consider this new activity.

We talked about the baby on her lap. She was just six months old, and I asked her name—which I promptly forgot when the woman looked up and suddenly exclaimed, "I can see the big E—and the two Es below!" This is when we both started to cry.

Next, she recognized her mother, who was approaching us from the opposite direction but was about the same distance away as the chart.

Then, at the sound of a twitter, she looked up and

said, "It's a bird!"

By this time, the mother was wrapped around us, and we all stood there crying tears of joy.

The next best experience I had was in the Ukraine. Our group of about thirty Lions flew into Switzerland, then boarded an out-of-date Russian plane, which didn't really look as if it would fly—in fact, I said a little prayer as we rattled along.

We made it safely to the capital city of Kiev, where we filled a comparatively modern bus with technicians and our luggage. We then rode all night to the Russian border.

We had snatched a couple hours of sleep on the bus, and after a cold breakfast on arrival at our destination, we went right to work. Actually, we didn't have a hot meal the entire two weeks we worked there, but we did make frequent trips across the street to a little shop serving hot coffee.

I had worked as an optician the previous forty-nine years and ten months, and it seemed like I'd had at least a hundred times the experience of any of the other technicians. We worked in a large hospital hall about fifty by 100 feet, lined with chairs, in which sat very large, very politely-waiting Ukrainian people.

It was the last day of our two-week visit, and we were starting to pack up, when a fellow came in carrying his daughter. She was about twelve years old, but very small, and she could neither walk nor talk. She seemed to be convulsive as well.

Our group was very tired, and we were practically out the door, but the girl's momma handed me a prescription so strong, we seldom even carried it. Without even looking, I reached around behind me and brought out a pair of glasses.

The frame almost exactly matched the color of the little girl's dress, and the prescription was as close as possible, as well. I fitted them to her small face.

She began to make excited noises and waved her arms in exuberance. Her daddy burst into tears, then her momma, and then me.

We hugged. All four of us were overjoyed.

Shortly after they left, I went outside and saw a beat-up, practically antique Russian automobile—in such bad shape I didn't think it would make it another five miles—with the family riding inside. The little girl saw me and waved with her fingers balled up in a fist. The poignancy struck me. I began to cry again. I wondered what those large-sized Ukrainian people thought of the large-sized American—I'm six foot four—with tears dripping off his chin.

In 2005, retired once more, I visited my friend who was the chairman of the Oregon Lions Sight and Hearing Education Foundation. He asked if I'd go to Pendleton to teach half a dozen young people—adult female prisoners—how to take the prescription off glasses using a Lensometer, then how to put them in a package, add the Rx number, and arrange them in correct order in fifteen or twenty boxes, three feet by one and a half feet by eight inches deep.

I worked with six women, five of which took and passed the state examination for optometry and are now working in the field somewhere in Oregon. The sixth one hoped to get the opportunity some day in the future.

For two weeks before I left, I also taught a willing friend, Ken Lockett, how to take my place.

Lions Clubs in the state of Oregon have collected at least 300,000 pair of used glasses. Because of their efforts, I was able to teach that first group of women, who, in turn, taught other women, so now at least twenty, probably more, are able to support themselves in the well-paying field of optometry.

I am so proud I can consider myself responsible for their beginning success.

"After 120 miles, she was marooned by a Blue Mountains blizzard."

Saga of Marie Dorion

John Terry

Some historians contend Marie Dorion deserves as much renown as Sacagawea. Maybe more.

"This remarkable woman was a much stronger person and played a much larger part in the development of Oregon than Sacagawea did, for, unlike the famed Lewis and Clark guide, Marie Dorion spent most of her life in this country," Bill Gulick says in *Roadside History of Oregon*.

In 1805-06 Sacagawea came with a company whose leaders, Meriwether Lewis and William Clark, were superbly equipped, mentally and physically. Marie, on the other hand, was with a group whose odyssey, in comparison, nearly makes Lewis and Clark's venture look like a picnic in the park.

They were about the same age. Sacagawea was a Shoshone. Marie's mother was an Iowan, her father, French-Canadian. Both married fur trappers: Sacagawea to Toussaint Charbonneau, Marie to Pierre Dorion.

Sacagawea trekked west with her infant son, Jean Baptiste. Dorion had two sons, Baptiste and Paul, ages four and two, when she started west in 1810.

That year, Wilson Price Hunt was in St. Louis organizing an overland expedition to set up a trading post at the mouth of the Columbia River, in the Pacific Northwest. Hunt and others were partners with John Jacob Astor in the Pacific Fur Company.

"Hunt wanted to enlist Pierre Dorion because of his knowledge of the country and tribes along the Missouri

River," Gayle C. Shirley says in *More Than Petticoats—Remarkable Oregon Women*.

Hunt agreed to pay Dorion $300 a year and gave him $200 in advance. Dorion, violent and villainous when drunk, undertook a celebrative binge and decided to pocket the advance and pledge allegiance to another outfit.

"The Dorion woman would not hear of this proposed act of treachery and told Pierre that they would join Hunt as agreed," biographer Jerome Peltier says in *Madam Dorion*. "During the quarrel that followed, the besotted Pierre struck Marie, who then proceeded to pick up a club and knock him out with a well-aimed blow to the head. She then walked out into the darkness with her bundle of belongings and her two sons."

Pierre, sobered and painfully chastised, relented. After making sure he was fulfilling his obligation to Hunt, Marie rejoined her husband.

"There is no record that Pierre Dorion ever attempted to beat his wife again," Gulick says.

On December 30, 1811, in the Grande Ronde Valley of (now) Eastern Oregon, the Dorion family lingered behind while Marie gave birth to a third child.

According to Washington Irving in *Astoria*, "In the course of the following morning, the Dorion family made its reappearance. Pierre came trudging in advance, followed by his valued, though skeleton steed, on which was mounted Marie with her new-born infant in her arms, and her boy of two years wrapped in blankets and slung at her side. The mother looked as unconcerned as if nothing had happened the previous night. The baby, gender unrecorded, died January 7, 1812."

"The best so far determined, is that the unmarked grave of this first part-white child born on what later became the Oregon Trail, was near Duncan Station, a now-vanished whistle-stop on the Union Pacific near La Grande," Gulick says.

They pulled into Fort Astoria on February 12, 1812. The Dorions were shortly dispatched to a trapping post in what is now southwestern Idaho.

In January 1814, Pierre was away when word came that hostile natives were about to attack. Marie took her sons and set out to warn her husband, only to find him and his party all slaughtered, except one man named LeClerc. She loaded up the badly wounded LeClerc and headed home. LeClerc died on the way.

Back at the post, Marie found all there massacred as well. She hurriedly loaded up some supplies and headed for safety. After 120 miles, she was marooned by a Blue Mountains blizzard.

"She slaughtered the horses and smoked the meat," Shirley says. "Then she built a hut of cedar branches, grass, and the horses' hides. For the next two months, mother and sons lived on horse meat, frozen berries, the inner bark from trees, and occasional mice and squirrels Marie caught in snares made of horsehair."

The weather broke in March, and Marie struggled to safety and the charity of a sympathetic Walla Wallas.

For the next quarter-century, she lived in that area. She married twice more, in 1818 to Louis Joseph Venier, with whom she had a daughter, Marguerite. After he was killed, she married Jean Baptiste Toupin in 1824. They had two children, Francis and Marie Anne.

Toupin worked as a Hudson's Bay Company translator at Fort Nez Perce (later Fort Walla Walla). In 1840 the couple moved to the Saint Louis area on French Prairie in Marion County. They were formally married in the Catholic Church, July 19, 1841.

Marie died September 5, 1850, and was buried beneath the steeple of the Saint Louis Church. The original log church burned, and the exact site of her grave was lost.

Plaques both inside and on the grounds of the present church honor her, as do the Madam Dorion Memorial Park near Wallula, Washington, and the Dorion Complex, a residence hall at Eastern Oregon University in La Grande.

John Terry's original column, "Saga of Marie Dorion," was published in the Sunday Oregonian, *8/14/05. Permission for the use of this story was given by* The Oregonian.

"...as they dove under us with more regularity, awe became genuine concern."

Watched by Whales

Jasmine Major

In the dark at sea, with our sight impaired, we found our other senses heightened. We could hear everything before we saw it.

We were about two weeks out of Hawaii on our sailboat, *Delphinus*, return bound to our homeport of Astoria, Oregon. In our search for wind, as the airs got light, we allowed ourselves to travel too far east, and we drifted—sails slack and flogging—in the fog and calm of the North Pacific High.

No wind, no engine, no visibility because of the dense fog. Thankfully, we at least had our solar panel and a waxing, nearly full moon. With our solar panel working days, we could power our electronics and cabin lights, but just before sunrise, not much charge was left.

During my watch on July 11, 9:00 p.m. to 12:00 a.m., I heard a deep exhale and the subsequent filling of a very large set of lungs. I could not see anything, just a ring of fog surrounding our becalmed vessel in all directions. Then I heard it again—unmistakably.

It was a mammal. It was too big to be one of the dolphins that sometimes lit up the ocean in a glittering display of bioluminescence as they played, jumping around *Delphinus*'s hull in the night. It had to be a whale.

From shortly after leaving Hawaii to this point in our voyage, we'd had an albatross, Albert Ross, accompanying us every day, no matter the weather. We had also been delighted by the friendly dolphins—our

48

vessel's namesake—and had seen large orcas not far off. One afternoon, my husband, Dean, had seen sharks thrashing something in the water—apparently lunch. But this animal was bigger.

The first night I just heard them. Nothing was visible. Dean didn't hear them. Then they started to surface early in the morning.

At first light, I could barely make out the long, black backs and small dorsal fins of the creatures that produced the profoundly deep breaths as they came to the surface to fill their lungs with air. There were at least three of them, maybe four—a small pod of whales— each at least forty feet long. Our boat was thirty-four feet long.

Soon they were appearing more regularly—each time, closer to our vessel.

After a couple of days of gradual approach and obvious interest in us, they began to surface just off our beam. They would fill their lungs, show their great backs, then dive directly under *Delphinus*'s keel, only to reappear on the other side.

We never knew when they were going to do this. But each time they did, they came closer and closer. At first it left us awestruck. But as they dove under us with more regularity, awe became genuine concern.

I found myself holding my breath and saying, "Dive! Dive! You know we draw six feet!" Then, in my adrenaline rush, I would be praying, "Please miss our keel! Please don't rub us!"

While at sea and far from assistance, there are several things that can prove life-threatening. All revolve around the necessity and success of keeping your floating home just that—floating. Gear failure, weather, and injury to the crew who operate the vessel, can each cause disaster.

Having experienced, not unexpectedly, mechanical failures our first week out to sea, we had become a true *sail*boat, as the use of our engine was compromised. However, we still had a sound rig, and the crew—Dean and I—remained healthy and well provisioned with both food and water.

Another less usual but very serious concern while underway is collision. A vessel can collide with a freighter, a stray container, or other large debris dislodged from a container ship. And, on occasion, whales have collided with vessels. This has become a more frequent problem with lighter displacement—faster sailboats usually designed for racing on the open ocean.

Delphinus is definitely not light displacement, weighing in at approximately fourteen tons. And we were anything but speedy. In fact, we were barely drifting with zero wind and no engine to move us out of our becalmed state. But, definitely, the whales posed a serious and potentially life-threatening concern for us.

Any collision would, unlike cases of those documented in sailing magazines, be not by accident, but from curiosity. Our whales were not aggressive, as far as we could tell—an aggressive whale could make enough of a show to make its motives quickly recognizable, even by amateur whale watchers such as we. But with the moon almost full, *Delphinus*'s canoe-shaped stern and full keel, her lack of mechanical sounds of any sort—we weren't even running the stereo in order to conserve electricity—must have seemed something of an oddity.

Delphinus's hull below the waterline was the approximate size and shape of a whale, unmoving, silhouetted against the full moon, and floating along the surface of the water for days. Any creature of intelligence might be intrigued—as were our whales.

About the fourth or fifth night, becalmed in the foggy outskirts of the North Pacific High, I was again on night watch—this time 3:00 a.m. to 6:00 a.m. I had just settled in with my blanket and hot drink. All was calm.

I heard a small dolphin come alongside *Delphinus* and could see it splashing about in the moonlight. I enjoyed the company.

Then I heard them—far off along the outskirts of the fog—a lap of water as they broke the surface, then, "Pwoooooooooh," the unmistakable filling of huge lungs.

They had been coming too close for comfort lately. I was not by any means pleased with their continued interest, especially on my night watch when my ears were already strained for any passing freighter, and my imagination freed to fill in any unknown blanks.

But they continued. "Pwoooooooooh," this one off our port stern. "Pwoooooooooh," that one off our port bow. "Pwoooooooooh," that one off our starboard stern.

They were all still a ways away. But as the minutes ticked by, they started to approach our floating home, staying in the same formation in relation to *Delphinus*, coming closer and closer—like a noose being tightened.

I felt as if I were being hunted. Uninformed as I was as to the identification of whale species and their migration patterns, I was still unsure as to whether these were gray whales, ocean-sized orcas, or some unknown variety. I was, in short, unsure as to whether these whales fed off krill and had large strainer-like mouths, or if their mouths were the sort filled with teeth used to eat fish, dolphins, and other small animals—of which I counted myself as one, were I to end up in the water.

"Pwoooooooooh. Pwoooooooooh."

I could see them! They were inside my small circle of visibility. My dolphin—although I had been glad of his company prior to our other visitors—again joined the scene. I was now unsure if he was potential bait or not, but seemingly unconcerned, he still did jump alongside the boat. He finally departed, none too soon, as the whales came ever closer, their interest remaining piqued.

My mind raced in the darkness. Should I be worried, or was I blowing this all out of proportion? Surely, they wouldn't knowingly bump into us. They were expert swimmers! This was their environment, and they hadn't touched us yet, but what if they became more curious or felt playful? It would only take one good nudge by something that large and powerful, and with nothing to steady us, no sails, no propulsion...

My nerves were worn, and every muscle in my body was completely taut. I couldn't take any more. I had to wake Dean. Sleep is such a precious commodity upon an ocean voyage, but I simply couldn't continue this alone.

The whales were now very close. I opened the companionway and called to my sleeping husband. At first, Dean was confused as I quickly explained that the whales were back. After all, we had weathered a tropical depression, the eye of a storm, and lightning encircling us 360 degrees. We had been kept below for three days through a gale, which brought us worse seas than the tropical depression, and I had carried on through terrible seasickness—weeks of it. Now, when all was calm, what could the problem possibly be?

Dean, half dazed with lingering slumber, clambered up from below decks. Still partially in the companionway, he asked, "How close are they?"

As if on cue, they surfaced. "Pwooooooooooh. Pwooooooooooh."

But this time, there was no straining to see them. As if petrified, we both stood in our places as we saw two huge whales surface within touching distance from where we were. We had only to reach out—to lean over just a bit. I didn't know how they could be so close without brushing our hull. One surfaced on the port side, maybe five feet from our hull, moving bow to stern.

Then during another breath, we saw the second whale, almost as close as the first, on our starboard side, stern to bow. Another deep breath followed. "Pwooooooooooh!"

"Go down below! Tether yourself to the boat," Dean ordered, needing no further explanation for my worried state.

We brought up the flare kit for a scrap of peace of mind—anything to help. Then Dean asked me for the bilge handle, a small metal handle that inserts into our manual bilge pump.

From the cockpit, Dean suggested that I turn on the radar to see if there were any vessels in our immediate vicinity that we could hail on the VHF. I switched on the radar, and we could hear the mechanical oscillating sound reverberate down the mast and through the hull. There were no vessels near us, but the whales were now moving away. They still circled around us. We could hear their breathing, but they were widening their course.

The small bilge handle proved our saving grace. By tapping the handle on the metal stanchions, we were transformed from an intriguing silhouette on the water to something mechanical, man-made—not part of the food chain. Whenever we stopped the tapping, the whales moved closer, always in the same relative formation. When we started tapping again, their orbit around us immediately enlarged.

At this point, Dean took over. I went below, wrapped myself in the fleece of the blanket on our berth, tethered myself to the boat, and relaxed into much-needed sleep.

When I awoke, it was daylight. It's amazing what sleep will do for your body and your morale! I found Dean in the cockpit—whales no longer circling—busy working on our cantankerous old engine. He fired it up just after I came above deck.

"Yes. Yes! Whoooooh! We have propulsion."

There was no one else to hear and no one to share this great triumph. We hugged ecstatically. Then Dean stood on the cockpit huffing and celebrating as though he'd just won a championship.

I couldn't stop smiling. I was so proud of him. This was one of those turning points in life—overcoming something, not giving up, never admitting defeat while we have breath to keep going.

We were 1,200 miles away from the nearest shore, just the two of us—motoring out of the calm, motoring away from our whales.

Later that day, we saw the clouds peel back like

cotton batting, rolling away to reveal a bright blue sky with lines of light mackerel clouds. We had wind! We raised the sails, cranked up Billy Joel on the stereo, and felt as if there were no place on earth we'd rather be.

Above our companionway hatch—sometime later that afternoon, sails up and sailing toward home—Dean placed over our companionway doors a small metal plaque, once a bookmark, bearing a quote from Winston Churchill: "Never, never, never quit."

We arrived at our homeport, the Port of Astoria, Oregon, eleven days and 1,100 miles later.

We replaced our engine later that year. After showing photographs to a friend who manages the local aquarium, he said our whales were probably a small pod of young, curious, and harmless gray whales.

"There's plenty of room aside the fireplace for your rockin' chair."

The Moving House

DeEtte Tetherow Guerin

A long time ago when I wuz just a young 'un, the house I wuz born in moved down over the hill to join with Grandma Nickerson's house. The two houses had been settin' bout half a mile apart.

Our house wuz the Tetherow house, and it wuz moved by our two big ol' horses, Coaley and Eagle. Coaley wuz black, and Eagle wuz white. The horses wuz hitched to rollin' logs.

Grandpa said, "*Gee!*" and the team brought the logs up in front of the house. Grandpa seldom had to say, "*Haw!*" for the horses knew when to stop.

Then Daddy unhitched them from the logs and hitched them to the house.

Grandpa said, "*Gee!*" and the big ol' horses strained mightily to pull the house forward on its rollin' logs.

Then the team went around behind the house with Grandpa to hitch up to the back logs, which the house had rolled off of, and bring them around front again. This went on for more than a week when Daddy and Grandpa wuzn't busy doing the other farm work.

Finally, the two houses wuz joined. And after all the sawin' and hammerin' and splicin' wuz done, there wuz four bedrooms upstairs and three down, besides the big kitchen and the bigger livin' room.

Grandpa George Washington Tetherow, who had always lived with us up on the hill, brought his clock and his rocking chair into the new livin' room in Grandma Nickerson's house that we wuz all to share.

Grandpa's uncle, Soloman Tetherow, had been captain of the Blue Bucket wagon train on the Oregon Trail back in 1842, when Grandpa George was eleven. Great Uncle Soloman wuz elected leader, partly because he wuz big and strong and smart, and partly because he wuz polite and civil.

My Grandpa George wuz also big and strong and smart and polite and civil too. He knew not to crowd people.

So he stood in Grandma Nickerson's old livin' room, and he said, "Mrs. Nickerson, ma'am, I'd be right pleased if y'all would allow me to set my clock on your mantle alongside your clock, and place my rocking chair t'other side of your fireplace."

Now Grandma Nickerson could be a mite cranky if any of the children wuz to be trompin' around in the garden pluggin' watermelons, without pluggin' them back up again—if they wuz too green so they'd go sour. Or if any young 'uns wuz to worry the pigs or tease her buggy horse, Barney. But she knew how to be polite and civil too.

Grandma Nickerson replied, "I'd be right proud, Mr. Tetherow, if you'd set your clock alongside mine on the mantelpiece. And there's plenty of room aside the fireplace for your rockin' chair too. Would you prefer the right hand side or the left?"

Since Grandma wuz already settin' on the left, he said, "I'd be much obliged to take the right hand side, ma'am." And so he did.

Grandpa Tetherow always wound his clock, and Grandma Nickerson always wound her clock, come Saturday night. They each set on their own side of the fireplace and never a cross word did they exchange.

DeEtte Tetherow Guerin was blonde, bright, and beloved. Born in 1906, she loved to help with everything, and she and her younger brother, Bill, did all the chores together. When DeEtte was only six, she and Bill got into a mud fight, and

56

both her eyes became infected. Before she started school, DeEtte was practically blind.

All of her life, DeEtte worked like a trooper. When she was in her late teens, she married Andrew Ocheltree, and they had a son they named Bill. In 2000, DeEtte passed away. She had outlived her four brothers, two sisters, three husbands, and her beloved son.

"My hair stood on end, and I began
to pray for deliverance."

The Longest Night of My Life
from the book, *Courage*

W. A. "Bill" Johnson

In 1960, I made the decision to re-enlist in the Army and make the military my career. Although I was unable to maintain my former rank of Master Sergeant, I felt I would be able to support my family on the pay of a Sergeant E-5. That decision made, I re-upped and was sent to a Repo-Depo—the place where you await orders and/or assignments.

There are only a few types of terrain no one is ever prepared for, such as, the extreme cold—the Arctic—the desert, or the jungle. I drew the jungle. In August that same year, I climbed aboard a troop transport with thousands of other military members headed for the Caribbean. We were in the midst of a military build-up for Castro and Cuba. My assignment was Panama. I was both apprehensive and anxious at the same time. After all, I'd never served outside the U.S., and I'd never been on a troop transport, either.

After disembarking from the ship onto the docks in Panama, we were met by an army officer and a number of five-ton trucks, complete with canvas tops. We were herded into the backs of the trucks—much the same as sheep or cattle—and hauled off to our new company.

The heat was beyond oppressive. I felt as though I'd never breathe again, and if the trip didn't end soon, I'd die. The trip eventually ended, and to my amazement, I didn't die. Although you couldn't have convinced me that I would at the time, I eventually acclimated and learned to love Panama.

After a number of assignments and attending a number of schools, I was called into the Company Commander's office. He told me each of the companies in the Battle Group had been asked to pick a soldier they felt would be able to satisfactorily complete a difficult school—Jungle Warfare Training Center (JWTC). He asked that I make him and our company proud.

I was soon on my way to more weeks in the classroom and then into the jungle. It was the experience of a lifetime!

The longest night of my life came in the midst of the escape and evasion portion of our training. Three hundred men from various countries and branches of the service had begun the school.

During a training exercise, half of us had been taken prisoner by the other half who were now considered the *"enemy"* and placed in detention centers. Next, we were supposed to escape in small groups, and with little more than a map and a compass, make our way through the jungle to a safe-zone, while avoiding capture by the *"enemy."*

I was the highest-ranking member of my group and was, therefore, in charge. After escaping, we rushed into the jungle, putting as much distance between us and the *"enemy"* as was possible. Once we felt relatively safe from pursuit, we stopped in a well-concealed spot, and with the map and compass, determined the direction we needed to follow in order to arrive at our destination and safety.

After traveling some distance through the jungle, we came to a hillside descending to a small river we would need to cross. This truly presented a problem.

First of all, the far side of the river was an ideal place for the *"enemy"* to be waiting, concealed in the jungle. If we waited for darkness, there was a high degree of likelihood we would be overtaken from behind and captured. Then, of course, there was always the possibility, however unlikely, a caiman—a relative of the crocodile native to South America—might be waiting for us in the waters below. Our choices were failure, or crossing. Since failure was not an option, there really was no choice. Therefore, we settled on a plan.

Since I felt it better for one of us to be captured than for all of us to be lost, I selected one soldier who seemed particularly fit and athletic and assigned him the task of going first, in order to assure a safe crossing for the rest of the group. If we were able to accomplish this, we would press on until our next difficulty. However, should we encounter the *"enemy,"* it was every man for himself.

Those able to avoid capture would make their way to the top of a large hill off to the left, on the far side of the river. There we would rendezvous and make new plans.

The *"enemy"* was far smarter than we gave them credit for. They allowed our point man to cross safely, scout around, and then signal for the rest of us to come ahead. The moment we reached the far side, they were on us like a pack of rabid dogs!

I found a jungle trail going off to the left and ran as though my life were on the line, not just my grade. I could hear at least two of the *"enemy"* on my trail. I ran to a bend, rounded it to where I was no longer in their sight, and jumped off the trail into a large clump of bushes, hoping against hope I wasn't going to land on a Bushmaster or a Fer-de-lance—both very poisonous snakes.

When my pursuers rounded the trail, they could no longer see me and stopped in confusion. They stood there discussing where I might be, and what to do. I, on the other hand, tried not to breathe—but felt I must sound like a steam engine.

Finally, after what seemed like an eternity, they left. I remained in hiding for some time, fearing a ruse—just knowing they were waiting for me to reappear. After I satisfied myself the silence indeed meant they were gone, I emerged from my hiding place and continued on toward the rendezvous point.

Upon arriving at the chosen spot, I was saddened to find I was alone. In all likelihood, it meant all of the others had again been taken prisoner, and I really was all alone. Believe me when I say my sadness was as much or more for me than for the others. It's no fun to be alone in the jungle, and even less at night—and night was falling.

There was nothing to do but make the best of an unpleasant situation. Something of a jungle trail ran down the spine of the ridge ahead. I took off my pack and laid it on one side of the trail to use as a pillow. I lay down on the trail, head on my pack, arms crossed, and machete in my right hand—in the event of need—and awaited total darkness and sleep.

Darkness came quickly. Sleep did not! If you've never been deep in a jungle under the canopy of the trees, you probably won't understand when I say, you can't see your hand in front of your face. The only thing I know that truly compares is being deep in an unlit cave where there is absolutely no light. If you're even slightly afraid of the dark and have an imagination, then pray to your maker you'll never be all alone in the jungle at night.

The dark settled over me quickly, and I'd just reached a drowsy state, brought on by total fatigue, when something rather small ran down the jungle trail, up one side of me, and down the other. I don't know what it was, but I'm fairly sure I sent it on its way with at least a hundred unsuccessful chops of my machete.

My nerves had barely settled, and I was again preparing to give sleep a try, when what I believe was a very large bat arrived determined to either drink my blood or have some other type of relationship with me. He didn't seem to want to quit flying in my face, but after another one hundred swings of my machete, he either left or his radar quit working, and I killed him.

My nerves were again trying to settle from the bat when I heard what sounded like a fairly large cat snarl or growl and a small animal screech. My hair stood on end, and I began to pray for deliverance. That was it! I certainly wasn't going to be able to sleep—and certainly not on the ground—so I began searching for an alternative.

I managed to find a break in the canopy where some light filtered through and saw a tree with a crotch that would allow me to get up off the ground. I placed my pack at the base of the tree and began to work my way up until I'd reached the first branch. Feeling rather smug and satisfied with myself, I began to look around. Imagine my horror when I realized there was a cliff jutting out to my immediate left that would allow a large jungle cat to merely walk up and—just standing there— partake of a nice, fresh, juicy army sergeant. In addition, no man alive can stand on one foot all night long in the tight crotch of a tree.

I was determined not to spend the night on the ground with the creatures of the jungle, and certainly not with what—in my mind—was a jaguar capable of dispatching me with little or no difficulty. Using the dim light coming through the filtered spot, I was able to see the neighboring tree went at least fifty feet up from the jungle floor and into the night sky. I could see what appeared to be a large number of branches, finger-like, forming what looked like a *"Tarzan"* resting place. This was the spot for me—my night's nest up above the jungle floor.

Making my way down to that tree, I placed my pack on my back and prepared to shinny up the other tree. At the time, I was in my mid-twenties and in the best shape of my life. I shinnied, and I shinnied to the point of exhaustion and knew I didn't have another shinny left in my body. Clinging for dear life, I looked up, and just above me, I saw a tree branch. I elected to grab for the branch. I don't know for sure what would have happened if I hadn't grasped it. Fortunately I did.

I pulled myself up onto the branch and prepared for the night. How Tarzan slept comfortably in tree branches all his life, I had no idea. I'm only glad I wasn't raised by apes. I'd rather sleep on rocks; at least you don't have to worry about falling out and killing yourself.

Each time I was able to obtain some degree of comfort and started to doze off, I would startle awake, finding myself about to fall out of the tree to my probable doom. In need of a solution, I settled on my ten-foot utility rope. I tied it to one branch, armpit high, and then wrapped it around all the remaining branches. This formed a sort of safety net, which at first, I thought, was going to solve my problem and allow me to sleep.

However, I quickly realized there was still a multitude of ways to slip between the rope and the branches and fall to my death. To prevent that, I took off my military belt and strapped my left arm to a sturdy branch of the tree. I wondered, had I fallen that night and ended up hanging by my left arm, unable to pull myself back into the tree, how scary would I look as a skeleton hanging there?

I did manage, from time to time, to actually fall asleep. I just prayed for the dawn and being able to get on with my escape.

In the early morning, I finally made my way to the safe-zone—after the longest night of my life.

W. A. "Bill" Johnson, graduated from Myrtle Point High School in Oregon, in 1954. Forty years later, single again, he reconnected with Shirley Davenport at a high school class reunion, and they were married a short time later. They are now enjoying spending time with their collective grandchildren and great-grandchildren.

"...no one believed she had written the tale of the monster."

Imprisoned!

Caprice

The heavy iron door clanged shut, the key grated in the lock, and the dungeon master shuffled up the stone steps after the last pilgrim. The darkness was complete.

"This is absolutely the most hideous idea you two have had yet," Mary spoke softly, but irately, as they stood hidden behind the pillar.

"You could have stayed back at the village and drunk grog," Byron pointed out.

"No, thanks—not with that leering innkeeper. I saw his bunch of hoodlums. Is the laudanum having any effect yet, Percy?" she asked her husband.

"I feel drowsy. I think I'll lie down here in this dry spot and go to sleep." Percy Byssus Shelley wrapped his cloak around him. "You can lie here beside me. With Byron on your other side you'll be warm and cozy."

"I hardly think warm and cozy is what I would consider this place, but I guess every bit of body heat would help." Mary, wrapped in her fur-lined cloak, sat down between the two men and listened—every nerve on end.

It wasn't long till the men fell into drug-induced sleep, snoring heavily. A rat scampered the length of the prison, past the leg irons, the rack, the many other instruments of torture, and over the legs of both men.

Mary shrieked. The men didn't stir. What a ghastly place, *Mary thought*. These really stupid men think they'll dream up hideous plots and make a fortune with their Penny Dreadfuls. *Aware of every sound, every squeak,*

64

every bat winging by, she shuddered.

Visions of horrible scenes of half-dead men hanging from the shackles on the wall, men strangling in ropes strung from the rafters, men tortured with red hot pokers heated in the great fire pots blazing along the prison floor passed before her eyes. Bodies were stacked like cordwood—the stench was unbearable. Mary's imagination didn't quit.

There was even a guillotine—the bloody basket adjacent held heads sliced and separated from the stacked bodies. A man on the rack moaned, then screamed in agony as the slats of the rack pulled ever farther apart. A cat o' nine tails cracked!

Finally, the night of terror ended, the two men struggled groggily to their feet, and just before noon, the three joined the tag end of a large group of people on their tour of the 3,000-year-old Castle of Chillon. This time—on the other side of the iron door—Mary was relieved to hear the scrape of the key and the heavy clang of the door opening that morning.

Back at Lord Byron's Villa Diodati, only a few days later, and after suffering a particularly heinous nightmare, Mary took quill in hand and began:

> *"It was on a dreary night of November that I beheld the accomplishment of my toils. I collected the instruments of life around me that I might infuse a spark of being into the lifeless thing that lay at my feet. By the glimmer of the half-extinguished light, I saw the dull yellow eye of the creature open; it breathed hard and a convulsive motion agitated its limbs."*

Thus began the early science fiction novel, *Frankenstein, or the Modern Prometheus.* Published anonymously in 1818, *Frankenstein* was an instant success. Mary was never able to write another novel as acclaimed. Later, after her husband's death, when her father had temporarily disowned her—for running off at sixteen with the already married poet, Shelley—she was struggling financially with two small children to support, and no one believed she had written the tale of the monster. After all, Mary was only a woman.

Mary Wollstonecraft Shelley had been much influenced by ghost stories told for amusement by the many famous and sophisticated visitors to Lord Byron's villa on the shore of Lake Geneva. She also later recounted the conversations of George Gordon, Lord Byron, and her husband—poet Percy Bysshe Shelley— in which they discussed reanimating corpses through the new science of galvanism.

According to the *Journal of the Royal Society of Medicine*, a Scottish physician, Christopher Goulding, also claimed Mrs. Shelley owed much of her knowledge of science to her husband, whose interest in medicine and chemistry had been fostered by an elderly mentor, James Lind, MD, who was one of the first people in Britain to conduct electro-medical experiments to make dead frogs jump like living ones. In the 1790s, he had privately suggested the use of electric shocks to cure insanity, after an audience with King George III—whom we remember well from our Revolutionary days—who suffered bouts of mental illness.

Dr. Lind's laboratory-study was described as having telescopes, galvanic batteries, daggers, electrical machines, etc. A friend recalled the rooms of the young poet Shelley at Oxford as filled with scientific clutter: an electrical machine, an air pump, a galvanic trough, a solar microscope, and a small glass retort above an argand lamp. Percy's reading list included Darwin and an account by Dr. Henry Cline of his resuscitation of a comatose sailor.

Because of the story I found in an ancient book, no one would have had to convince me that Mary Shelley was the author of *Frankenstein*. Around 1985, I volunteered to integrate a small college's collection into the vast shelves of the library of Santa Barbara. I'm an inveterate reader and was absolutely compelled to open every book, and at least leaf through it, reading a page here and there.

I came upon a fragile volume—small and once a beauty—and read every page. It was a story written by Mary Shelley of the night she actually hid with the two drugged men in the basement prison of the Castle of Chillon. The tome fascinated me, and I checked around to secure myself a copy. It was, of course, long out-of-print. But, an appropriator of rare books discovered the title listed in an English shop and said he could order it for me—for $48. I wish now I had succumbed. I have forgotten the date and name, but to this day, I yearn to own it.

Had I been Mary Shelley, I certainly could have written *Frankenstein*. I well remember her description of that dreadful night in the basement prison of Castle Chillon. The feelings of horror she felt in that place are the same feelings I felt over 150 years later. It was the late 1950s. I was in Switzerland on a tour of the continent when I happened upon a handbill announcing—in French—the reopening of the 3,000-year-old Castle Chillon's dungeon, "For those Brave Enough To Attempt..."

I thought I was brave enough.

The guide carried a flaming torch. The darkness of that huge dank basement was relieved only by that flickering flame. We saw chains, shackles, fire pits, pokers, battle-axes, scimitars, the rack, a kris, and every other cruel device invented by depraved men. The use of each instrument was carefully explained and some were demonstrated. A record was even played—by some unseen assistant—of groans and shrieks. Volunteers were requested to try out the rack. No one stepped forward.

I did not attempt to hide myself, with or without an accomplice. And I was so glad to hear that huge heavy iron door slam behind us, the rusty key grate in the lock. I understand exactly how Mary Shelley felt—and she had been only a year or so past sixteen. She had to be the author of *Frankenstein.* The dungeon tour of Castle Chillon firmly convinced me.

But, that was not the end of my experience. For sometime after the tour, I relived all the squeaks and scuttles, all the recorded sounds of depravity from the ghastly record. Had they been recorded at an actual site? The sickening appearance of all those instruments of torture, the lurid descriptions and disgusting demonstrations—all stuck in my brain and played the sights, the sounds, the clammy touch of the walls, and the fetid smells, over and over again.

I dreamed those feelings night after night. I thought I would go mad, until finally, I escaped from the continent of Europe to England, where a friend I had met on the ocean liner coming over from America, invited me to stay a few days with her in London in the middle of October. I was so glad to see her—a solid, most sensible woman with not a lick of imagination about her.

Margaret greeted me warmly. After a filling up with a late afternoon tea of sandwiches, topped off with a delicious lemon curd, she and I discussed the affairs of the world over a cup of Bigelow's green tea from a box of bags I had harbored in my luggage as a gift from America, for just such an occasion.

Margaret was delighted with my gift. She carefully placed both our tea bags on separate little receptacles to be used again in the morning—but that shouldn't have been surprising. Though The Great War had been over for more than ten years, the British were still terribly frugal—to the point of seeming stingy. Rationing seemed to be ongoing in England. I don't know that they actually still had ration books. I didn't ask.

Margaret mentioned, "Unless you know the butcher personally, it is strictly hamburger for you. But then, you wouldn't understand," she said. "You Americans are so spoiled."

I tried not to take offense, because everywhere I had gone on the continent, and now in England, everyone murmured, "She's an American. They're all so spoiled."

Although I hated then to admit it, we are. We think nothing of running a full tub of hot water or taking long showers. We expect a new paper bag for everything we buy. We often don't bother to eat the crusts on our bread and don't even force our children to. We sometimes throw out leftovers, and we don't save slivers of soap. All of the above, I'm sure, would be considered coarse by Margaret.

Actually, I'm sure of it, because, although the evening became quite chilly, she told me, "I'm sorry it's a bit nippy tonight, but we never turn on the heat until November."

She carefully ran a metal hot water bottle with a handle like a broom's, the length and width of my bed, and brought in a pitcher of hot water and a white washcloth and towel, embroidered with a crest, for me to use with the Spode basin which sat on the polished commode. I exclaimed to Margaret about the crest, and she did modestly admit to it belonging to her family. Her great, great, grandmother had been a lady in waiting.

I did sleep well in the feather bed that night. I had left the ghosts on the continent.Although there was an electric heater in my room, I did not touch the controls in the morning—after all, it wasn't near November. I didn't want to be remembered as, "that really rotten, spoiled American."

Back at home in the U.S.A., I save my slivers of soap. Sometimes I use my tea bag twice. But while I keep my thermostat set between seventy and seventy-five degrees—I *don't* wait until November to turn it on.

One more series of incidents does come to mind from my time overseas in the '50s. I purposely sailed to Europe on the *Liberté* because of the beauty of the ocean voyage, and also because a French ship would surely have French passengers. I wanted to polish my French.

My opportunity came when I was seated at a table with a most charming Frenchman. He had been visiting his daughter and her American husband in North

Carolina and was heading home. His name was Antoiné, and he was everything a Frenchman should be: handsome, knowledgeable, gallant, and with exquisite table manners.

Antoiné was more than willing to help me with the French language. He improved my use of verbs and enlarged, considerably, my vocabulary. He seemed very happy in my company, and I in his.

At the table, and also in our deck chairs, we worked on my French. But the voyage was long, and we often simply conversed—in a combination of French and English—as I helped him with his English, as well.

At the end of the voyage, Antoiné asked if I would like to visit him some evening near Christmas in Paris. I agreed that would be lovely.

Then he asked, "Or are you staying that long? Or when do you plan to depart?"

"I'm not sure, exactly. I guess I'll leave when I have seen everything there is to see. I have no set schedule."

"You don't? But what if you should run out of funds?"

"I'd just wire home for more."

"You can do that? Incredible!" he said, in French.

"Of course. Can't you?"

"But, no. We are only allowed to take $20 out of the country with us. And that is all—no more! You Americans are so spoiled," he commented, ruefully.

Oh—the evening in Paris was unforgettable, including the ride from the airport in Antoiné's little Citroen, through holiday rush-hour traffic.

You haven't lived—or almost died—until you've survived rush-hour traffic in Paris! Unless you've experienced a soiree with a debonair and romantic Frenchman.

"...a massive dark object popped out of the night sky a few feet away— heading straight for us!"

Perilous Voyage

Dale Rue

Toward the end of March 1974, I walked through the side door of the Happy Inn Restaurant and made my way toward the bar where my friend Harvey sat drinking. He waved me over, bought me a drink, and introduced the two men sitting at his table.

"Dale, this is Bobby. He owns a fishing boat and is looking for a crew. This is Roger, and he works on the boat."

I shook their hands, pulled up the empty chair, and said, "Tell me more."

Harvey was all excited and told me he had signed up as navigator. He kept reminding me I had nothing better going on and that I should also join the crew. After several hours of steady drinking and sea stories, I reluctantly agreed to be their new deckhand. What I knew about fishing would have easily fit in one of our empty shot glasses.

Several days later, I showed up at the dock looking for a boat called *Kusco*. I saw a boat matching its description and hoped that wasn't it. I knew very little about boats, but *Kusco* looked tired, and her faded white paint and rusty cables and winches were not reassuring. Harvey was there on the dock visiting with Roger, who had helped pilot *Kusco* to Astoria from California and was waiting for his paycheck.

Bobby jumped off the boat to greet us, and then he

headed for the bank. Roger had agreed to help Bobby re-crew the boat. Now that he had fulfilled his agreement, he would return to his family in California. He said he would not be going with us.

I was surprised Roger had bought a ticket on another boat back to California instead of sailing with us, especially since *Kusco* had been short on crewmembers. I listened carefully to what Roger was saying, and then I asked him about Bobby.

Nervously, Roger looked up and down the dock, back up toward the road, and then began to tell us a different story from the one we'd heard at the restaurant two days before.

Roger told us, "I need to get paid, and I can't afford to piss Bobby off, but you guys need to know what you're getting yourselves into."

He told Harvey and me that he'd hired on as navigator and deck boss. He explained Bobby had purchased the boat a few years before with $25,000 he'd borrowed from his grandmother. He said *Kusco* was built in 1910 for the squid fisheries around Mexico and California and had recently been converted for tuna fishing. They'd sailed it from Los Angeles with a brand new crew.

"Aside from Bobby, I was the only experienced fisherman on the boat," Roger continued. "Bobby hired me because he doesn't know how to navigate. The rest of the crew were all greenhorns, just like you guys.

"We were following the tuna fleet north. Everything was fine for the first few days, then, off the Oregon-California coast, we had a Bermuda Triangle kind of experience. A heavy fog rolled in, engulfing the boat. We were swallowed up and could not see a thing. Our compass needle spun like a top, and we had no idea where we were.

"The radio didn't appear to be working properly. The waves picked up, and we found ourselves at the mercy of the sea. I've had my share of weird experiences in the past, but that time, I was really afraid. The water around us was dark brown and boiled with tuna. Thousands of them were roiling and jumping out of the water. We managed to get ourselves out on the deck and tried jigging, but the fish wouldn't bite. The entire experience was surreal. I often wonder if the cook had put LSD in our food. It was too weird to undergo without drugs."

I wasn't sure what to make of Roger or his story. I looked at Harvey and then back at Roger as he went on.

"Our trip started out peculiar as hell. That should have been my first warning, but I blew it off. Our new cook returned from grocery shopping with $2,000 worth of sauerkraut. I was dumbfounded.

"Bobby had sent him to buy groceries for our trip north to Oregon. He didn't buy anything else—no bread, no meat, no milk—not a damned thing aside from sauerkraut. We were supposed to stop later to re-provision, but instead, we exhausted what canned goods we had."

Roger related that when *Kusco* finally arrived in Oregon, just outside of Astoria, it was around midnight, as Bobby had missed one of the channel markers, and they grounded on a sandbar.

"When we ran aground, the boat flopped over on her side, and seawater flooded the engine room, knocking out the main generator. We managed to get a call off to the Coast Guard before everything went dead, and we were holding on to the side of the boat when they arrived.

"After getting everyone safely off the boat, the Coast Guard towed *Kusco* to the shipyard for repairs. I landed in the hospital with pneumonia. The rest of the crew scattered."

Roger added that Bobby was a serious alcoholic and addicted to speed. He noted, "Bobby has trouble making sound decisions. I found his drug stash three days ago and flushed it down the toilet. You guys should be okay."

Almost immediately, we saw Bobby drive up and park. He had a young guy with him who looked to be about eighteen. My mind was racing, and my throat was dry as beach sand. I looked at Harvey, and we sucked in our breath. I didn't have time to talk to Harvey or even to think about what we'd just been told.

Bobby walked up and handed Roger an envelope. The two shook hands. Bobby introduced the new man, Danny, to the three of us. Danny was our last crewmember.

We all said our goodbyes to Roger, and he walked away. Bobby grabbed Danny's backpack and helped him climb on board. Then, he looked at us and said we would be leaving right away. Bobby fired up the engine and waved to me. I untied the dock lines, tossed them on board, and jumped on.

Kusco was a sixty-foot, sixty-ton, faded white wooden-planked boat with its name painted in faded black letters above the wheelhouse windows. It was stubby, with a sharply-pointed bow. A large rust-colored anchor winch filled most of the space up front. The braided bowlines hung limply from the winch's capstan.

The deck leading to the stern was about three feet wide and worn from years of foot traffic and weather exposure. The stern had two small winches, a deep-sink, several workstations, and a mast with floodlights overhanging a second deck. The second deck had a steering station and provided storage for a three-person aluminum lifeboat. There was an emergency life raft nearby in its weathered fiberglass storage pod.

Halfway between the bow and stern was a large plywood superstructure with a wooden door. On the inside were two portside bunk beds next to the captain's quarters. Up towards the bow and to the right were a steering station and large compass. To the left was the boat's galley, or cooking area, containing a diesel-fuel stove and a small refrigerator under the counter.

The eating area was attached to the portside bulkhead about ten feet from the door. Constructed of plywood, it had under-seat storage. The wooden tabletop was attached to a pedestal bolted to the floor.

Between the table and the refrigerator was a two-foot by two-foot, one-inch thick plywood trapdoor recessed into the floor. Below the trapdoor was a four-rung wooden ladder descending into the engine room. An antique diesel engine supplied the power and was the heartbeat of *Kusco*.

The boat's auxiliary generator was just past the engine, and to its right was a sectioned-off area of the bow called the forepeak. It had a sliding door and was the main storage area. There were coils of deck line, fishing jigs, tools, spare anchor chain, hardware, and assorted odds and ends. There was an odd, musty smell that reminded me of engine lube, wet burlap, and fish. This was also where I would be sleeping.

While we crossed the bar, I headed below to get some seasick pills from my quarters. As I dropped down through the hatch, I was alarmed by what I saw.

Hot engine oil was being flung from the main engine everywhere. There was oil dripping from the overhead beams and running down the walls. The floor was so slippery I could hardly stay upright as I ran to get Bobby. He poured fresh oil down the engine filler spout and yelled out over the scream of the diesel engine that we could shut down once we were across the bar and out at sea. Then we could figure out what was wrong. I laid on my sleeping bag to ease the nausea and dozed off.

A short time later, I awoke when I heard the engine shut down. I tugged my shoes on, pulled open the door, and stepped into the engine room. We must have crossed the bar, because *Kusco* was drifting in the ocean, and her engine room was quiet.

Bobby was busy, bent over the main engine. He had a small socket wrench in his hand. He looked at me and said, "Someone at the shipyard installed the damn valve-cover gasket upside down."

I scrubbed oil off the overhead walls and floor as Bobby made repairs and put things back together. We were shut down and drifting for several hours.

Early the next morning, I awoke to the sound of

metal rattling. I looked the engine over and then made my way topside. I heard Bobby cursing as I crawled through the hatch.

"What's up, Bobby?"

"Oh, the damn autopilot just broke, and our steering chains have piled up in the stern. We are dead in the water. It is going to be a bitch to fix!"

Somehow we needed to fish 120 feet of chain through the three-quarter-inch metal conduit and then reconnect the two ends of the sprocket at the steering station up front. Ten hours later, we had finally retrieved the chains on both sides and reattached the separated links with a chunk of wire and called it good.

The next day around 4:00 p.m., I pulled my first work shift and joined Danny up on the flying bridge. He and I would be working the 4:00 p.m. to 8:00 p.m. and 4:00 a.m. to 8:00 a.m. shifts together. Danny was from Ilwaco, Washington, and told me he had fished one summer on a charter boat with his grandfather. I told him I didn't know anything about fishing and even less about boats.

We watched day turn into night and enjoyed one of the most beautiful red sunsets I have ever seen. The story, *Jonathan Livingston Seagull,* blared from the ship's radio as we steered *Kusco* south on the heading Harvey had given us.

The water was flat calm—not a breeze anywhere. The blood-red sky soon faded, and a thousand stars came out to play. The moon seemed to vanish as the sea reflected the stars above. It was hard to tell where the horizon stopped and the night sky began. The temperature dropped, and it became quite cold.

Off in the distance, I saw the red and green running lights of another vessel. We were about fifty miles off the Oregon coast. The approaching lights grew larger, and it was obvious that something would be passing us before long.

Bobby had told us that red running lights were always on the port or left side, and that green running lights were on the starboard or right side of all boats and ships. He'd also told us that approaching vessels generally pass one another on the port side. It's referred to as going port-to-port or red light to red light.

We watched the oncoming lights grow nearer, and I began feeling uneasy. I knew they were headed in our general direction, but we couldn't get a fix on their exact course. The lights appeared to be crossing us on our right—or was it our left? We changed our heading a few degrees, but the lights continued their mysterious dance.

The star-reflected ocean provided little information, but by then, we were sure that the lights heading our way were on an approaching ship. Next, the red light became obscured, leaving two green lights, which seemed to grow larger and farther apart as they approached. I became confused and a bit disoriented.

I knew our two vessels were getting close when the overhead stars seemed to disappear, and I thought I saw a moving shadow. I held my breath. My heart was beating wildly, and my eyes and ears strained for any sign of motion.

There was the sound of rushing water, and then a massive dark object popped out of the night sky a few feet away—heading straight for us! Its green running light towered thirty feet above us as its reflection danced off the water. There was absolutely no sign of life. I could easily have thrown a rock and hit it.

I yelled at Danny, "I think they're going to run over us!"

Danny yanked the wheel hard left and sounded our air horn as the monstrous black ship slid by our starboard side in the frigid air.

The enormous ship blocked the starlit sky and was completely dark, except for the one green running light and its reflection. It appeared as if the ship was running itself.

We couldn't see the propeller, but we heard the ka-chunk, ka-chunk, ka-chunk of her giant propeller blades ripping through the water as her massive hull slid by our bow, nearly sinking us in the process. Time seemed to stop as she slipped by us and disappeared into the night.

Around 7:30 a.m., close to the end of our next morning's watch, the marine radio weather report notified all mariners of a thirty-five to fifty-knot, southeasterly storm brewing. According to our chart, we were headed straight for it. I ran down and shook Bobby awake. He was groggy, but he sat up on his bunk as I gave him the scoop.

He said, "Aw, hell, the storm will pass before we're even close." Then he lay back down, and that was the end of the discussion.

The next morning, around 3:45 a.m., I made my way topside to relieve the other watch crew. Harvey was by himself at the wheel. Bobby and Danny were in their bunks sound asleep.

I made my way toward the galley stove, holding on to anything I could to steady myself. It was all I could do to remain upright. Huge waves slammed into *Kusco*, fully catching my attention. I held the edge of the counter for support as the boat became swallowed up in the sea and was battered by wave after wave.

We had apparently hit the storm head on, and we were losing ground. Harvey estimated we had been blown at least fifty miles out to sea, and we had lost all our electronics and communications. We were somewhere off the coast of Florence, Oregon. The trouble was just beginning.

The windows were all steamed up. You couldn't see a thing. Our deck lines, and any unsecured gear, had washed overboard, and it was a miracle they hadn't tangled in the propeller. There was a four-inch-long brass storm-latch attached to the doorframe that held the door open for ventilation. The fresh air helped de-fog the windows a little, but it also let in saltwater spray that soon covered the linoleum where we were walking.

Our navigational charts were stored in a plywood bin screwed to the ceiling above the door. I stood peering out through the crack as Harvey walked behind me to change charts. A giant wave hit us broadside, causing Harvey to lose his footing on the wet floor. He slammed into me with his full weight.

A few weeks earlier as *Kusco* was undergoing shipyard repairs from capsizing in the Columbia, a welder had made the decision to attach a new handrail to the boat's gunwale, just outside the galley door on her starboard side.

For sixty-four years, there had been no handrail— only a sagging, three-foot-long galvanized chain that could be dropped when loading supplies onto the boat. The new handrail saved our lives that night. When we slammed into the door, the force of our combined weight split the two-inch-thick, oak frame door from top to bottom. Once the wind caught the loose door, it ripped it from its hinges, flipping it across the waves like a Frisbee. I watched it disappear into the night.

My chest hit the new handrail first, and Harvey landed on me. The force of the impact cracked my ribs and left me completely stunned. I tried desperately to hold on as waves began to wash me towards the stern.

I reached out, but my hand slipped on the wet rail. I was losing the battle, when Harvey grabbed my feet and pulled me back through the open door frame. I scampered up under the table and held on for dear life. Harvey ran back and grabbed the wheel as the rest of our crew slept, unaware of the dangerous situation we were in.

As I lay there under the table, I remember looking up at the ship's barometer, mounted on the wall in front of me, and randomly thinking, "Now I know how boats go down." I wondered if our bodies would wash up on some beach, or if they would be found at all. I felt sorry for my grandparents and my sister once they heard the news of our drowning.

I could see straight outside where the door had been, and I was terrified at the sight. Enormous waves were crashing into the boat as seawater poured in through the open door frame and accumulated on the floor. In a moment's time, the water was a foot deep.

The refrigerator door popped open, and its contents washed back and forth on the floor at my feet. The TV broke loose, landing on the table above my head, and crashed to the floor, becoming part of the watery mix.

Time seemed to stop. I hurt all over. I couldn't stop thinking about my family. I prayed like there was no tomorrow, but must have passed out, because the next thing I remember was waking up to the smell of smoke. It was morning, and the storm had passed us by. Harvey was up on the flying bridge and still on watch.

I made my way outside and looked up at him. "Harvey, I smell something burning!"

Then I woke up Bobby and told him I smelled smoke. We did a quick once over in the engine room and looked around outside but didn't see anything. Bobby blew it off, suggesting it was my imagination.

Just then, a large smoke plume and a two-foot high flame popped out of the floor next to the galley table. Smoke engulfed the small room instantly. I dropped through the hatch to the engine room looking for a clue. The flames seemed to be inside the wall where the exhaust was located. In no time, I became overwhelmed with smoke and ran outside for air.

I'd remembered seeing a fire extinguisher in the galley and several in the engine room. With a wet rag over my face, I ran back inside, grabbed the galley extinguisher, and pointed it at the flames—but it was empty. I located the other two in the engine room, but they were empty as well.

I called to Danny, "If we can't put this fire out, it will burn to the waterline!"

I grabbed a fire axe and sunk it into the plywood bulkhead as deep as I could as Danny did the same with the backside of a claw hammer. Then, we ran outside for more air. Harvey couldn't see what was going on and kept asking us for an update. I couldn't talk because I was choking from the smoke.

He finally slowed the boat down to an idle and

Perilous Voyage

cranked the wheel hard left. Then he began climbing down from the flying bridge. With the wheel turned to the port side, the boat started going in a large circle. At one point, the smoke sucked out through the open door as quickly as it had appeared. It was as if a large vacuum fan had been turned on.

I yelled at Harvey, "Keep us on that course!"

He ran back up the ladder and headed us in the direction I'd indicated.

Once we had the smoke under control, we went after the fire. Danny and I ripped huge chunks of three-quarter-inch marine grade plywood off the walls until we located the fire inside the main wall beams—which were glowing cherry red. The two of us formed a bucket brigade and dumped seawater on the fire until it was extinguished.

Meanwhile, Bobby was running around like a headless chicken, holding the boat's paperwork in one hand and his pocketknife in the other, planning to cut our lifeboat loose. He yelled at us for tearing up his newly painted walls, but we kept at it until there was no sign of fire.

During the storm, several tons of ice we'd had stored in the hold broke up. Since the bulk of our groceries were stored with the ice, our bilge pumps became clogged with hamburger meat, and we couldn't pump out the extra water we'd taken on.

Additionally, the fuel tank equalizing valve that pumped fuel simultaneously from port and starboard fuel tanks became defective, causing the boat to pump all its fuel from the portside tanks, and us to list heavily to the starboard side. All our communications had been knocked out, leaving us with just our wheelhouse compass and one very dim flashlight. And that's the condition we remained in until we arrived in Monterey, California, several nights later.

When we were tied securely to the dock in Monterey, I jumped off the boat and kissed the dock. I had no intention of returning to sea. I would give Bobby

81

the news the next day. My life had miraculously been spared, and I wasn't about to push my good fortune.

The next morning, I walked up the pier to find a doctor to get a chest X-ray. Danny searched for a pay phone and called home. He and I returned to the boat about the same time. Bobby saw us coming and informed us that we would be leaving soon, heading for Los Angeles.

Danny told Bobby his grandmother was very sick, and he had to leave immediately. He grabbed his gear and left like a bat out of hell.

I told Bobby I was done and was donating my hip boots, sleeping bag, and clothes to the boat. He was really upset that we quit with no notice. I didn't care. I wasn't about to go back onboard *Kusco*.

I waved to Harvey, untied the deck-line from the cleat, and tossed it to Bobby. I watched as they made their way out of the harbor in the mid-morning sun and turned south. Once the boat was just a speck on the horizon, I turned and walked up the pier. It felt wonderful to be alive!

Dale Rue moved to Alaska a few weeks later and lost touch with Harvey. Many years later, he heard that Kusco's *main engine had blown up about ten hours after departing Monterey. The boat was towed somewhere for repairs. After his crew experience on* Kusco, *he well understood why Roger had not returned south with them. Dale said the* Kusco *voyage changed the course of his life.*

"They had Chief running back and forth through the house, leaping from couch to chair to table..."

Forever a Blackberry Goat

Pat Williams

While I was face painting one weekend at the Astoria Winter Market, I met an eleven-year-old vendor. She was homeschooled, and she raised goats, made goat milk products, and was an awesome salesperson. She asked if we could barter something for me to paint her face.

I said sure, and after I'd given her a full-face painting of a Toggenburg goat, she showed me several items, including greeting cards with pictures of goats on them. I chose one that closely resembled our goat, Chief—a Nubian wether that our son, Shawn, had gotten from his 4-H leader, Doris.

One of the nice things about Doris Warren being the leader of the Dairy Goat 4-H club was, kids who didn't live on acreage could still have the experience of working with farm animals. They could use Doris's goat kids to learn how to handle the animals and then show them at the 4-H Fair.

After Shawn showed Chief in both the county and state fairs when he was in junior high, Doris mentioned something about butchering the goats shown that year. Shawn pushed the panic button. No one was going to put his Chiefy in the freezer!

There was nothing else to do but swap some chore time for Chief's life. Next thing I knew, we were loading a young, between four- and six-month-old goat into the back of our station wagon to take home with us.

All I could think along the way was, "How in the world am I going to explain this to Bud?"

When we got to the house, I dropped the boy kid off with his goat kid. I then told Shawn to watch Chief while I went to the feed store to get some goat supplies. About an hour later, I came home and was a little concerned when I didn't see Shawn or the goat in the yard.

As I opened the door to the house, I could hear Shawn and my other kids laughing. Then I saw why. They had Chief running back and forth through the house, leaping from couch to chair to table and back again.

This came to an abrupt halt when I explained that a goat was a farm animal and just peed and pooped wherever it felt like it. Needless to say, Chief was suddenly returned to the great outdoors.

Next on my list was a goat house, and Doris had told us where she thought we could get one. By the time I went south of town a few miles to a farm, picked up the A-frame goat house, got Chief settled in his new place, and had him fed and watered, it was almost time for Bud to come home from work. Chief chewed his cud during the introduction to the head of family. The man of the house grumbled, then grumbled some more, then went and had a beer and tried to forget about the "damn goat."

Over the next few years, we had lots of fun with Chief. He and Shawn took part in dairy goat showmanship several more times before Shawn's interests changed and Chief became just another member of the family, though he did have one important job—he kept the blackberry vines in the backyard under control.

Two incidents involving Chief have always given our family a chuckle in retrospect. Both of them involved our neighbor lady.

The Abrahams lived right behind us, and they had five children in their family, like ours. Whenever their mom, Roxie, wanted one of them to come home from playing outdoors, she would—like all the rest of the moms in the neighborhood—go out on her front porch and loudly call the child she wanted.

Almost immediately after getting Chief, we all noticed something rather weird. Whenever Roxie called for Arlene, Jeanine, Richie, or Mindy, there was no problem. But, when she called for Gary, Chief immediately called back. This made it impossible for Roxie to know whether her son had answered or not. No matter how many times she called Gary's name, Chief responded.

The other incident had to do with snakes. Roxie didn't like them, and before she'd go out into the yard, she'd send her little dog scampering around to make sure the snakes had been scared away. What Roxie didn't know was that Shawn had witnessed an older boy killing every garter snake he found in the neighborhood. So, to protect them, Shawn was collecting snakes and turning them loose in our backyard, just a hedge away from the Abrahams' front yard.

When I realized this, I reminded Shawn of Roxie's aversion to snakes and asked him not to keep bringing them home. Unfortunately, he continued to sneak every snake he could find into the yard. Of course, they scattered to the four winds.

Roxie mentioned a couple times that there seemed to be a lot more snakes than there had been a year or two before. I scolded Shawn, but it didn't seem to really do any good.

This all changed one day when Shawn was in the backyard with Chief, just hangin' out. Shawn was sitting on the back steps playing with something and talking to Chief—who was grazing—when suddenly, Chief's head jerked up in surprise.

Then just as suddenly, Chief snapped his head forward, grabbed a garter snake in his teeth, and gave it a vicious shake. He then flung the dead reptile about six feet away and resumed munching on the grass.

Shawn was in shock! He came running into the house to report what Chief had done. Man, did I ever think quickly how to use it to good advantage. I told him, he had little choice. He'd have to gather up all the snakes he could find, take them across the dike, and turn them loose in the woods.

For once, I got no argument. For the next few weeks, Shawn spent a lot of time snake hunting and making sure Chief didn't get his teeth on any more of them.

Several years later, Animal Control informed us that goats were farm animals and needed to live on farms, not in town in a backyard. So, we found Chief a home out in the country as chief blackberry vine trimmer.

After he left us, we checked on him several times. He was obviously happy and moving on with his life, so we eventually lost track of him. I am really glad he spent those few years with us, and so glad Chief didn't end up packaged in white butcher paper in Doris's freezer.

"Our uphill hike was slow and arduous..."

There's Gold in Them Thar Hills

Shelley Cabell Moore

My dad, Rodolph Warrington Cabell, Jr., had always wanted to visit his grandfather's family homestead and gold mine in Cabell City, Oregon, and his stories about it instilled the same desire in me. So, in 1985, my husband, Roy, and I made a date with my parents to take a trip there and look for remains of the La Bellevue Mine founded by my great-grandfather and great-grand uncle.

On a sunny Saturday in July, the four of us packed up their four-wheel drive Subaru wagon and left Seattle on our vacation. We headed south through the desolate countryside of eastern Washington, where we saw nothing but scrub-brush for miles. We crossed the mighty Columbia River dividing the states of Washington and Oregon and made our way down through the farmlands of central Oregon. There, we drove mile after mile past fields of waving grain.

It was an all day trip to the eastern side of the state, and we got a motel when we finally arrived in Baker City. The next morning, rested and satisfied after a nice big breakfast, Roy, my parents, and I spoke to some local people and got directions to the uninhabited Cabell City. Eagerly, we headed off to see the family ghost town and cemetery.

What greeted us on our arrival were only a couple of dilapidated, boarded up buildings and some old mining equipment that must have been left behind when the operations ceased. The cemetery was a short walk away, and we were able to locate my great-grand aunt's gravestone among the gravesites.

From there, we took a Forest Service road to try and locate my great-grandfather's old La Bellevue Mine stamp mill, but we were only able to drive up a short way because a tree had fallen, blocking the road. We decided to walk on from there to continue our search.

Since we were up in the mountains, and the area was known to have snakes, Mom refused to get out of the car and chose to stay there and wait for our return. When she was a young girl, some neighborhood boys pinned her down on the ground and taunted her mercilessly with a snake—face to face. Then, to make things worse, she got on her bicycle one day and began to ride, only to feel something hitting her leg with every cycle of the spinning back wheel. When she looked down, she discovered it was a garter snake that had wound itself in the spokes, and she virtually flew off her bike to escape it. For some time after that, even pictures of snakes in books or magazines frightened her. One time when Dad took her on a date to the movies, a snake appeared on the screen, and Mom practically jumped into his lap.

Needless to say, we didn't argue with her about staying behind. Dad, Roy, and I began the trek on up the mountainside to see what we could find. Our uphill hike was slow and arduous, as the narrow dirt road rose at almost a forty-five degree slope. It was also a very dry, sunny afternoon. Both of the men were having little trouble with the climb, but I was tiring quickly, and the heat and steep ascent were really getting to me. Finally, I just had to stop and rest.

I spotted a small pool in the creek running below us, alongside the road. I asked Roy to wait for me while I went to catch my breath and splash on some of the glacial water to cool myself off.

I made my way down the dusty, rocky slope, and when I got to the creek, feeling hot and sweaty, I had an overwhelming urge to sit in the water and wash off all the perspiration. Dad had gone on ahead, but just to be safe, I asked Roy to stand guard. I stripped naked, gingerly stepped into the clear, rocky-bottom pool, and slowly immersed myself until I was up to my neck in the chilly water.

My skin tingled as my body temperature cooled, and I felt thoroughly refreshed. With only the sounds of birds chirping and trickling water, I lay in the pool, gazing up at the clear blue sky, completely relaxed and enjoying the quiet, peaceful moment. Then, it hit me. I was having my first ever experience with skinny-dipping—and loving every minute of it!

Once I was fully revitalized and rejuvenated, I leisurely stepped out of the pool, stood by the edge of the creek, and let the warm, fresh air, bright sunshine, and gentle breeze dry the water droplets on my body. After I dressed, I clambered back up the slope to rejoin Roy, and we held hands and laughed at my impromptu side trip as we continued on the extensive, steep trail to catch up with Dad.

We found him standing in the road, looking up at what little remained of the old Cabell stamp mill's framework, large waterwheel, and long narrow sluice after nearly a century of weathering. It was rotted and in ruin, but our imaginations kicked in to see it whole and running, cleansing the ore concentrates back when our ancestors, John and Fred Cabell, worked the La Bellevue Mine.

My great-grandfather, John Breckinridge Cabell, was born in 1850 in Virginia and came out to Oregon with his older brother, Fred, in or about 1875. By 1885, they had acquired a large piece of property in the high desert region of Eastern Oregon. It was located in the mountains, about eleven miles north of the town of Granite, not far from Baker City.

They both homesteaded there, and the area where they opened the La Bellevue Mine became known as Cabell City. It wasn't really a city by today's standards—just an encampment with housing for the mineworkers and buildings to house the mining equipment.

Fred and his wife, Johanna, had a daughter in the late 1880s; sadly, their child died from an unknown illness at the age of six. Fred, Johanna, and their little girl are buried in the Cabell City cemetery, but as we found out during our visit, only Johanna's headstone is still readable.

My great-grandfather met and married my great-grandmother in Baker City in 1890—when she was seventeen and he was forty—and they lived in a cabin near the La Bellevue mine. They had my grandfather, Rodolph Warrington Cabell, Sr., in 1894. Roy and I have a photo hanging on the wall in our home of my one-year-old grandfather in front of the Cabell cabin. It was taken in the early summer of 1895, when a dusting of snow was still on the ground. Rodolph is being held on the back of a jet black horse by his father, and his mother and his Aunt Millie are standing beside them in their long-sleeved floor-length dresses.

The Cabell brothers owned and operated several mines, and they built a stamp mill on a hillside near the La Bellevue Mine that used a wood powered steam engine to run it. By the early 1890s, John and Frank had hired workers to operate the mill, cut wood for the steam engine, and haul the concentrates—unprocessed gold ore—from the stamp mill to the railroad in Baker City.

It was a rugged, three day round trip to the railroad, with a team of four horses drawing the wagon. The hauler was paid fifty cents per 100 pounds of concentrates, and he usually hauled about 3,000 pounds per trip, earning about $15 for his three days of work—a lot of money in those times.

The nearest town was Granite, and it had a post office, a nice large hotel, two general stores, and a blacksmith. Groceries and other supplies were delivered to Cabell City and the five mines in the area from the general stores, and the mail was delivered by horseback.

Since the La Bellevue Mine was situated at over 5,000 ft. in elevation, the Cabells wintered over at the Granite Hotel each year. The mine could only be worked for a little over four months, from late June until early November, due to snow.

John and Fred made a living with their mines, but the two brothers never struck it rich. Unfortunately, my great-grandfather was injured while working the La Bellevue Mine in 1901. He pulled a kidney—which couldn't be repaired in those days—and died from complications. He was fifty-one years old.

The La Bellevue Mine was sold to a mining company after John's death, and my great-grandmother left the area with her son. Little Rodolph was only seven years old when he lost his father.

Once he was grown, my grandfather got a law degree, fought with the Oregon National Guard Cavalry in 1916-17 against Pancho Villa on the US-Mexico border, and was a captain in the Army Chemical Warfare Service during WWI. From his time in the service, we have his riding crop, his Colt 45 pistol, his bayonet, and a hand crank gas alarm that he bronzed.

After the war, Rodolph went into the shipping business in Portland, Oregon, starting out as a checker on the docks. He married my grandmother when he was thirty, and she, twenty-two. My grandfather met her at the general store in Rhododendron on Mt. Hood and gave her a ride home—and the rest, as they say, was history.

He worked his way up in the Portland shipping business to owner and Chairman of the Board of the International Shipping Co. His company did most of their business with Scandinavia before WWII, and with Japan and Greece after the war. Rodolph finally retired at age eighty-eight, and he died at age ninety-three in 1987.

Roy, Dad, and I and gazed together at the remnants of my grandfather's childhood home on the hillside near the stamp mill, and I inhaled deeply, tired from the remainder of our hike. I could almost see baby Rodolph there on the black horse's back, his father's strong hands holding him securely and his mother and aunt next to them, standing stoically in front of the cabin. It was so inspiring to be in a place of such historical relevance to my family—and the history of Oregon.

After taking some photos of the ruins of the mill and the Cabells' cabin, the three of us walked back down the dirt road to the car where Mom was *somewhat* patiently waiting. I told her we hadn't seen a single snake on the way up or down.

On our way back to Baker City, we stopped by the Ranger Station to ask if there were any more Cabell family sites in the area for us to visit. The ranger was very friendly and helpful—he even gave us a local Forest Service road map and showed us the road that came in at top of the mountain, just above the La Bellevue Mine stamp mill.

It turned out that we could have avoided the long climb we'd made to get there, if only we'd stopped at the station on our way *in*! But, then I would have missed out on my little adventure in the wilds of Eastern Oregon.

Shelley Cabell Moore was born in Oregon City, Oregon. After graduating from Oregon State University, she married her high school sweetheart, Roy, who became a test engineer at Boeing. Shelley taught elementary school for sixteen years before their daughter was born and she became a fulltime mom. She enjoys spending time with her family, reading, writing, and traveling to experience different countries and their cultures. Shelley and Roy currently live in the greater Seattle, Washington, area.

"The deck and bulkheads oozed with the scent of past conflict..."

The Battleship's Last Mission

Dan Butler

I could tell that Captain Don Hughes was captivated by the *USS New Jersey* from the moment he stepped aboard. Gazing about the deck with an elated grin, he whispered a word I would always associate with the giant battleship, "Awesome!"

It seemed rather ironic such an enthralled comment would come from a man who was no stranger to either the Navy or large ocean-going vessels. Even after having served at sea during the Second World War, sailing as commanding officer of a navy destroyer, and working for over thirty years as a Columbia River pilot, Captain Donald E. Hughes was totally captivated by this huge Navy ship.

It was June of 1990, and we were about to embark from San Diego on *New Jersey*'s last official mission to Portland, Oregon, where she would be the star attraction of the Rose Festival fleet. Captain Hughes would have the honor of piloting the battleship up the Columbia River on what would be her final voyage.

Immediately following this trip, *New Jersey* would return to San Diego for decommissioning. Within several years, her three Iowa-class sisters would also be retired. Two of them would slip into the silent oblivion of mothballs, and two—including *New Jersey*—would be preserved as floating museums. For ship lovers, Navy buffs, and the thousands who had served aboard these imposing dreadnaughts, their passing was not without a sense of loss as significant icons of American maritime, fading into history. It was virtually certain these magnificent vessels would never again steam across the seas in our defense.

Decommissioning any naval vessel can be a melancholy event. The mothballing of these unique ships was especially poignant to me, as I'd had the great fortune to sail with Captain Hughes on *New Jersey*'s last trip. This is the story of my adventures on her final voyage, and the closing chapter of one of our country's most decorated warships.

Arriving at the San Diego Naval Base, I felt like we had stepped through a time warp when we came to a sign boldly stating: **Battleship Country.** Just beyond the sign towered the real-life version of the ship I'd only seen in history books: the USS *New Jersey*, or as the Navy designated her, the BB-62.

Spotlessly clean and freshly painted, *New Jersey*'s enormous superstructure sparkled in the warmth of the midday sun as multi-colored signal flags fluttered over the stacks. Bridge windows looked sternly down to the main deck and across the massive guns that pointed ominously at the horizon.

She was, as Captain Hughes would so eloquently remark, "Simply awesome!"

Built during the peak of America's industrial might, *New Jersey* and her sisters—*Iowa*, *Missouri*, and *Wisconsin*—were the epitome of the phrase "biggest and best." Everything about them was massive.

At 887 feet in length and 108 feet wide, they were just barely narrow enough to squeeze through the Panama Canal. Their nine sixteen-inch diameter guns could throw a ton of high explosives twenty-three miles with deadly accuracy.

Steel armor plating encased all vital areas of the ship. Around the conning tower, it was almost eighteen inches thick. Four eighteen-foot high propellers combined into 212,000 horsepower to move the 57,000-

ton ship forward at over thirty knots—a knot is 6,080 feet compared to a mile's 5,280 feet.

While both the US Navy and world merchant fleets have ships that have more cargo capacity and are bigger in size and weight, faster, and more glamorous, none have the ominous mystique and lethal sleekness of an Iowa-class battleship. The four ships in this class provided a textbook image for the term battleship.

Although she appeared somewhat reduced in scale—being moored between two hulking aircraft carriers—*New Jersey* was still a behemoth. Unlike the carriers, the Big J looked like a warship was supposed to look, in the classic sense, with her long, tapered bow stretching majestically beyond a solid superstructure bristling with weapons, radar, masts, and twin stacks.

With two massive turrets forward and one aft, her decks were dominated by the menacing presence of her nine sixteen-inch guns. Yet, in spite of her formidable and serious business persona, the ship's hull lines flowed gracefully with balanced, well-proportioned dimensions topside.

While most modern Navy vessels have all the aesthetic appeal of a shoebox, the Iowa-class battleship had an air of stately elegance. Clearly, *New Jersey* was the grand lady of the fleet.

Stepping off the gangway and onto the solid expanse of the teak-covered main deck, I was thrilled to the point of gawking. I could hardly believe I was standing on an Iowa-class battleship, and I felt like the proverbial kid in a candy shop. Somehow, I stifled the urge to yell, "WOW!"

While waiting for an officer to escort us to our quarters, Captain Hughes and I perused a large display plaque outlining the ship's service record. Reading down the long list of deployments, bits of World War II naval history flashed from memory as I recognized the names of famous events occurring long before my time. I'd only imagined the great battles of the Leyte Gulf and the Philippine Sea, the typhoon of 1944, Admiral Halsey and

Tokyo Rose—but this was where the stuff had actually happened.

All around me, the deck and the bulkheads oozed with the scent of past conflicts, which had taken place around distant islands with strange sounding names. I could almost feel a distinct presence and hear the murmur of voices from the thousands of men present during those thunderous battles. A shiver ran down my spine.

Lost in the ship's historical ambience, I was snapped back to present day reality when I overheard an officer mentioning someone had neglected to secure quarters on the ship for me. They assured me they'd scrounge up something.

I smiled and said, "I'm not particular. I can sleep in the chain locker if necessary." Just being aboard was all that mattered.

As Captain Hughes was escorted away to a cabin in Officer Country, I assumed I'd get a berth somewhere deep below in the crew's crowded space. Much to my surprise, the officer who led me through the ship began climbing up, ladder after ladder, until we reached a cabin high in the 06 level of the conning tower.

The compartment, temporarily vacated by the ship's PR officer, was next to the navigator's cabin six decks above the main deck. It was even higher than the navigation bridge on the 04 level. I had, in fact, been given the uppermost berth on the entire ship! Although it was a cramped, windowless, and tomb-like compartment with an incredibly heavy watertight door, these were privileged accommodations as far as I was concerned.

Don Hughes and a couple of other river pilots from Portland were aboard at the request of New Jersey's Commanding Officer, Ronald D. Tucker. Captain Tucker had wanted the pilots to observe the ship-handling characteristics of the battleship before he'd feel comfortable bringing his ship nearly 100 miles up the narrow, winding, and relatively shallow Columbia River to the Portland harbor. Although the pilots routinely handled ships larger and deeper than *New Jersey*, Captain Tucker was the boss, and he was adamant on this requirement before anyone would be allowed to pilot what he considered as his "national treasure."

As the river pilot's dispatcher, I'd spent the previous year on the phone assisting the ship's navigation officer, Lieutenant Pat Curtis, with their upcoming visit. When I heard about the pilots being invited, I quickly asked if I could tag along, recognizing it would be a once-in-a-lifetime opportunity to go to sea on an American battleship.

Later that evening, we walked the weathered yet immaculate decks up to the sleek bow and stared back at the extraordinary ship looming in the night sky. The massive guns, lit from the side with the warm glow of shore-side lights, jutted up from their turrets against the imposing silhouette of the darkened superstructure. The tropical night air was still—other than the soft lap of water against the gray hull and the faint hum of machinery from deep within the ship.

A sudden volley of smoke erupted from one of the stacks as engineers fired off boilers in preparation for the morning sailing. The slumbering battleship stirred to life for one more mission. I savored the time we spent on the bow that night, just soaking up the scene and recognizing we were witnessing the final wake up of a great naval vessel in the twilight of her career.

It was a moving, almost reverential experience inspiring one of the pilots to remark, "This is like being in church. It seems we should whisper."

Repeating his initial impression, Captain Hughes shook his head with a quiet chuckle. "Awesome."

The next morning found *New Jersey* bathed in brilliant sunlight, steamed up, and ready to sail. After breakfast, we attended the daily weather and navigation briefing in the wardroom as Captain Tucker outlined to his officers, in terms leaving little doubt, what he expected from them on this last assignment.

Just prior to getting underway, the captain addressed the crew over the ship's public address (PA) system. "Although we're going to a pleasurable port, this is not a pleasure cruise. We have important drills and training to perform which we want to do right, and above all, safely. This will be The Battleship's last mission, so we want her to look her best. That is all."

We soon discovered Captain Tucker was fond of referring to *New Jersey* as The Battleship. It was his way of setting his ship apart from "those other battleships" in the Iowa-class with less distinguished service records. Even though the famous USS *Missouri* was far better known to the public, the BB-62 was actually the most decorated active ship in the Navy—with fifteen battle stars—and the only ship to be commissioned four times.

It was apparent that the crew, like their captain, also took a lot of pride in serving on The Battleship. No detail seemed too small as they tackled everything from painting and polishing to removing seagull droppings on top of one of the gun barrels.

The daily schedule of ship's activities, called the Plan of the Day, set the tone for her final voyage with the title, "The Battleship: Going Out in Style."

When the tugboats finally began to assist *New Jersey* from her berth, I stood watching with excitement as the big ship was turned slowly around for the short trip to the ocean. We were surprised with only a smattering of pleasure boats and well-wishers that showed up to see the ship off. Being a Navy town, San Diego takes a rather ho-hum attitude when it comes to fleet sailing—even if it is a battleship.

Portland would have a totally different response. We had already assured several young and eager sailors, the city of Portland would indeed be as receptive as was legendary to the navy's annual visit. One of the Rose Festival's most popular events was the arrival of the fleet. The news that the largest Navy ship to ever attend was coming would surely draw tens of thousands.

Standing atop the navigation bridge on the 05 level, I

watched as the ship began gliding effortlessly through the harbor. It was a truly magnificent sight. *New Jersey*'s fresh gray paint and polished brass fixtures glistened in the sunlight.

The ship's crew, decked out in their white summer uniforms, manned the rail—providing a stunning contrast over the sparkling blue waters of the bay. A Marine color guard stood at attention atop turret number two, just behind the giant sixteen-inch guns, as the Stars and Stripes flapped gently in the breeze.

I couldn't help thinking that if this scene didn't conjure up patriotic feelings of American strength and pride, nothing would. It was obvious why no ship afloat had ever been better suited to "showing the flag" than the New Jersey and her sisters. Evidently one of our pilots had similar thoughts and remarked, "Kind of makes you glad you're a citizen of this country, doesn't it?"

Climbing up to the 08-level maneuvering bridge, I joined Don Hughes in an out-of-the-way corner to watch Captain Tucker and his "ship drivers" at work. After clearing the bay and dropping off the harbor pilot, the crew was released to quarters as the ship headed for sea.

With her long bow passing Pt. Loma and pointing toward the open Pacific, it didn't take much imagination to visualize what it must have been like in the 1940s to be underway to meet the unseen enemy and do battle across the ocean.

Almost unnoticed at first, the long Pacific swells started flowing under the bow. Feeling the ship beginning to rise beneath my feet, I began to appreciate the term "WETSU" that I'd noticed on jacket patches and the ship's flag. The word was the Captain's personal acronym that, roughly translated, meant: "We Eat This Stuff Up."

Turning to Don, I murmured under my breath, "I can't believe we're doing this."

He smiled and nodded in silent agreement, obviously just as thrilled to be aboard *New Jersey* as I was. Having worked with the Navy for nearly two years, encouraging them that it would be possible to bring the ship to Portland, this was the reward for his efforts. For me, a childhood dream had just become reality. I was on the bridge of a US battleship at sea!

As we left the bridge to head below, one of the officers took our visitor ID badges, saying, "Well, now that we're at sea, you won't need these anymore. You've got the run of the ship."

This was incredible!

We had the privilege to dine in the spacious officers' wardroom running nearly the full width of the main deck. Before the trip, several of our associates back home scoffed at the idea of volunteering to spend four days with the navy and eating their chow.

"Who'd wanna do that?" they laughed. "The only thing they'll feed you is wieners."

Well, maybe on some ships—but the chow they served up in *New Jersey*'s wardroom was not only filling, but was generally very tasty. As we sat down to this well-prepared food available in large quantities, we had to chuckle, "Oh, no—wienies again!" This became the standard remark at our table for virtually every meal.

Enjoying the appetizing food, and participating in the camaraderie of the wardroom while the battleship moved steadily through the ocean, prompted me to consider whether I'd made the right career choice many years ago. It was just as I had read. There really is no better duty than battleship duty.

On our first afternoon at sea, I was content to amble about the decks, watching the ship sail through the windy, azure waters off Southern California as we passed by the San Clemente Islands. I found an excellent sightseeing position on the unused 03-level flag bridge. When *New Jersey* served as flagship, an admiral and his staff occupied this deck—but on this voyage, it was deserted.

It felt a little strange climbing up into the big chair and settling down between its cushioned armrests. This was the same chair used by Admiral William F. Halsey during WWII when the ship was his flagship for the Third Fleet. I marveled at the historical perspective of observing the ship at sea from the exact spot the admiral had, and tried to picture what he might have been contemplating during those uncertain and stressful times. I could feel why some still referred to it as Halsey's chair.

That evening, as the sun blazed its way into the tossing horizon, the wind became fierce enough that the officers on watch secured the main deck, as it was beginning to be lashed with sea spray. Off in the distance, we could see some of the other ships of the fleet, which had now joined us for the trip to Portland.

It was perversely satisfying to watch the dim silhouettes of smaller destroyers and frigates pitching violently through the growing seas as *New Jersey* plowed ahead with stolid indifference.

A lone sailor standing at the rail pointed with casual pride. "Look at the ride those guys have. That's why we call The Battleship a Cadillac."

When I finally turned in late that first night at sea, I couldn't help but feel snug and secure in my bunk high in the ship's superstructure. Although history has proved time and again no ship is invincible to the sea or foe, riding a US battleship in the open ocean has got to be about the safest, most comforting feeling one can have afloat. Even with *New Jersey*'s size, the seas caused a definite rising and falling, but it was a steady, deliberate movement. It didn't matter much to me because I almost immediately drifted off into cozy slumber as the wind howled around the darkened ship.

On our first full day at sea, Don, the other river pilots, and I got to observe several training exercises. The first involved an "attack" by two land-based F-16s, appearing out of nowhere and screaming overhead as air defense crews attempted to knock down the intruders.

One of the Big J's gun-director crews was ecstatic when it was able to lock onto the attacker for what would have been a potential kill. This was accomplished using some of the ship's vintage equipment, which said as much for the high degree of training and skill of the crew as it did for the fifty-year difference in technology.

The main event of the day was a fleet gunnery drill. Our only disappointment of the entire voyage was that the ship's big sixteen-inchers could not be fired, pending the outcome of an investigation into the USS *Iowa*'s turret explosion, which had killed forty-seven men.

Captain Tucker had asked his superiors for a waiver on the moratorium, as he felt completely confident with his guns and gun crews. The crew was also eager to fire the big guns because, as one sailor told us, "It'd sure be a lot easier to fire those shells than having to offload them when we get back."

But it wasn't to be. Only the five-inch mounts would be fired. For this drill, all the ships formed up into a single column with *New Jersey* in the lead. Locating a great vantage point on the 04 level, I stood just aft the bridge and directly above the forward five-inch gun mount on the starboard side—with my camera ready.

Even with ear protection, Lieutenant Curtis warned me, "Say, Dan, it might be a little loud here."

I didn't care. Having never seen a gun of this size fire before, I wanted the closest front row seat I could find. I wanted to fully experience these guns in action, and besides, they couldn't be that...

"KABOOOOOM!"

Geez Louise, what a sound! The gun had fired with such a tremendous blast of flame and ferocious noise, I didn't have to decide when to take a picture, as my startled reflexes squeezed the shutter release.

We'd been told the five-inchers had a much sharper report than the sixteen's deep boom, but I was totally unprepared for just how violent the concussion would be. So was Hughes—as the batteries flew out of his video camera and scattered across the deck. It was the loudest noise I'd ever heard.

The other mounts began a series of consecutive

shots in a thunderous and extraordinary display of firepower. Far off on the horizon, towering explosions of water were faintly visible as the rounds tore into the Pacific.

I was completely thrilled to be a part of this and kept grinning as I thought, *WETSU! WETSU!*

At the conclusion of the exercise, there was a final, ceremonial firing of all six of *New Jersey*'s five-inch mounts. Captain Tucker stood on the 05 level atop the bridge with two remote firing mechanisms in hand to personally do the honors. A small group of watch-standers and onlookers gathered as he squeezed the buttons. Simultaneously, the ship's guns all erupted with a fiery blast and collective boom.

It was over much too quickly, I thought.

Evidently, so did the captain, as he smiled and commented wryly, "Well, that was fun. Maybe we ought to do that again."

But The Battleship would fire her guns no more. Walking aft, we looked across *New Jersey*'s wake to watch the other ships in the column fire their weapons. With a belch of flame, and the distance-delayed thump of exploding powder, the ships pummeled the blue waters as signalmen flashed messages through the haze.

As the show's symphonic theme played in my head, I thought, *This is far better than watching the old TV series, "Victory at Sea."*

During the four days we were aboard *New Jersey* steaming up the coasts of California and Oregon, we had the rare opportunity to explore the ship from the forward windlass room to the aft steering compartment. We became fairly proficient in navigating the maze of passageways, ladders, and spaces that made *New Jersey* a self-contained city for over 1,500 personnel. We sampled a real flavor of life aboard a battleship at sea by being able to observe the drills, attend lectures for midshipmen, visit with the crew, and listen to the nightly briefings.

Although I found that the ship's high-tech

communications, missile launchers, and fire control gadgets were certainly interesting, most of these devices could be found on any modern warship. For me, it was far more impressive to see the original equipment making *New Jersey* and her sisters unique. I was intrigued that much of the "low-tech" systems on the battleship were functioning and as effective in the 1990s—a definite tribute to the design and workmanship going into building the Iowa-class ships.

Of course the main attraction for most visitors to The Battleship is the business end—the nine sixteen-inch guns mounted in twos which weigh as much as a locomotive, and the primary purpose for their existence. They came close to being the largest guns ever mounted aboard a ship—only the Japanese Yamato-class battleships had larger eighteen-inchers.

These huge guns were not much different, in theory at least, from the cannons used in the days of sailing ships. Critics would employ this comparison to argue the battleship's guns were "primitive weapons." Yet, a standard charge of 660 pounds of powder could propel a 2,700-pound projectile to targets twenty-three miles away with devastating force.

In spite of *Iowa*'s fatal tragedy and regardless of the cause, the *New Jersey* gun crews we talked with were totally satisfied with the safety of their weapons. This confidence was born out of their training and forty years of experience firing many thousands of rounds without problems or injuries.

Another area especially fascinating to me was the gigantic steam plant powering the ship, which we had the special privilege of touring while underway. Due to crew reductions and fuel-saving measures, the ship steamed along at a leisurely fourteen knots with only half of her eight boilers lit off. At full power, the four engine rooms could propel the 57,000-ton ship forward at thirty-five knots.

The officer who took us through the fire rooms and engine spaces was genuinely proud of the plant, a trait common to all the engineering personnel we talked to. Much of their pride stemmed from the fact that these engine rooms had more original equipment intact and operating than any other component or system on the ship.

These were the same boilers and engines installed when the ship was launched in 1942, still performing admirably almost fifty years later. Again, this fact was not only a function of quality design and construction, but also a testament to the crew's ability to operate and maintain the ship.

While it was fairly hot and noisy below deck, the engine rooms on *New Jersey* were as spotless as the rest of the ship, with the controls, valves, piping, and gauges all in immaculate condition.

The four huge screws were driven by four main engines, each consisting of a high- and low-pressure Westinghouse steam turbine geared to a single propeller shaft. That these turbines continued to spin in the 1990s certainly gave credence to their manufacturer's slogan, "You can be sure, if it's Westinghouse."

Another fascinating piece of "original equipment" we found aboard was ex-*New Jersey* crewman, Frank Blair. Frank was considered a "plank owner" since he was a member of the first crew after commissioning and had served as the ship's dentist in 1943. He had been active as a *New Jersey* alum for years, and his participation in this trip, and his recollections of those early years, added greatly to our enjoyment and education.

After four days at sea, we saw our first land on June 6, as *New Jersey* slowed at the sea buoy off the mouth of the Columbia River to rendezvous with the pilot boat. With the bar pilot aboard, The Battleship began to move against the flow of the West's largest river.

I had watched the bar pilot board and then stepped back inside. When I returned topside a short time later, I was surprised to find land no longer visible. The narrow bow was pointing back to sea.

We soon learned some protestors from Greenpeace were dangling from ropes beneath Astoria's 205-foot-high Megler Bridge connecting Oregon and Washington. Apparently, they didn't want *New Jersey* to visit with her alleged nuclear arsenal.

As local law enforcement attempted to remove them, the ship steamed in slow circles outside the bar. After two hours of fruitless negotiation, the protestors remained but assured the police they would not drop onto the ship or try to board.

Captain Tucker kept the crew informed of the situation over the ship's PA, stressing it was their right to protest and that his main concern was for the safety of both the ship and those hanging below the span. He then gave orders to start into the river toward Astoria and the bridge.

Privately, the captain was not very amused. He puzzled with a personal irony, "Hell, I've even sent money to those people to help save the whales."

Passing by senior ex-crewman Blair, Captain Tucker muttered, "This kind of stuff happen back in '43, Frank?"

Frank just smiled.

After an anxious couple of hours, the tension peaked as the bridge finally loomed overhead with all hands taking cover off the open decks. Easing slowly beneath the protestors still dangling from above, the big ship passed without incident and the crew gave a collective sigh of relief. The Battleship could now begin the last leg of her trip up to Portland.

Finished with his assignment, the bar pilot left by launch, and Captain Hughes took over as river pilot, skillfully directing the New Jersey through the 600-foot-wide channel under the watchful eye of Captain Tucker.

Hunkered down in his captain's chair on the drafty, open-air maneuvering bridge, the Commanding Officer chewed on his ever-present swizzle stick, relieved to be past the obstacles in Astoria but restlessly anticipating the remainder of the transit. Looking through his binoculars, the captain was genuinely amazed at the growing number of people gathering along the highways and banks to watch *New Jersey*'s passage in this seemingly remote and unpopulated area.

As we glided by the large paper mill at Wauna, Captain Tucker sat up in his chair. "Look at that," he remarked incredulously. "There are people watching from every door and window in that building!"

"Just wait till we get to Portland." Hughes smiled knowingly.

At an especially narrow portion of the river, *New Jersey* met an ocean-bound Japanese car carrier named the *Toyofuji No. 14*. This close and somewhat symbolic passing of the two vessels, each built during vastly different periods of world history, seemed to suggest both ships had been successful in their respective missions. Still, such a chance encounter with an Iowa-class ship about four decades earlier would have had a profoundly different outcome.

Our time warp aboard The Battleship ended abruptly with her arrival at the Port of Longview, Washington, where she tied up for the night. Faced with the desirable dilemma of finishing the trip on board or watching from the riverbank, I opted not to ride since it had been impossible to view the ship in her entirety while underway.

The next morning, hundreds of lucky passengers boarded *New Jersey* for the short trip up to Portland. Armed with a camera and portable radio, I watched from the Oregon side of the river with dozens of sightseers and media people.

Suddenly, Don Hughes's voice crackled over Channel 13. "This is the USS *New Jersey* preparing to depart Longview Berth No. 5 for the Portland harbor. *New Jersey* out."

As the ship moved slowly into mid-stream, she seemed strangely out of place in a river accustomed to the passage of bulky merchant vessels loaded with logs, grain, and cars. It was also surprising how she appeared rather average in size compared with some of the supertankers and container ships frequenting the river.

I overheard some local river-watchers making similar observations, with one commenting, "I thought the battleships were supposed to be really huge. What's the big deal?"

But it was a big deal. Not only did *New Jersey* look magnificent as she approached and steamed majestically past, but this was also the first, and no doubt, last time a U.S. battleship would visit the river. No other ship in Portland's history had ever drawn such media attention, as evidenced by the hundreds of people lining the shores and the thick flotilla of small craft gathering to greet the ship.

During her five-day visit in Portland, over 40,000 people toured *New Jersey*—most of them realizing it would be their only chance to see an active battleship.

At the conclusion of the Rose Festival, the fleet sailed with my wife and me riding *New Jersey* one last time from Portland to Longview. Although most folks were no doubt excited to be aboard, for me the gray skies and scattered showers reflected a somber sense of parting.

With no longer any "official" reason for being aboard, my access was restricted to the wardroom and lower decks—just like the rest of the nearly 600 passengers who made the trip. Like them, I was merely a visitor, and The Battleship was no longer "my" ship.

The next morning, I boarded the tug *Portland* as it assisted *New Jersey* off the dock and turned her down river. From there, I followed her passage by car to Astoria, where I went out on the pilot launch, *The Peacock*, to deliver the bar pilot and pick up Captain Hughes.

It was thrilling as the launch deftly maneuvered alongside *New Jersey*'s massive hull, flowing effortlessly along through the water. After quickly taking a couple of photos, I reached over and touched the solid gray steel wall. She was alive with movement. Immediately struck with the sentimental significance of the moment, I recognized this would be the last time I'd ever witness the ship under her own power.

With the bar pilot aboard, Hughes carefully climbed down the Jacob's ladder to the launch. As the boat pulled away, *New Jersey* sounded two loud farewell blasts from her steam horn and quickly increased her speed.

Although a veteran of thousands of similar river transits, Captain Hughes's weathered face wore a boyish grin. Pausing only to throw a wave in the direction of the ship's bridge, he promptly fired up his video camera to record The Battleship's departure. Don was clearly delighted to have played a key role in the success of *New Jersey*'s last mission.

By the time we reached the dock, *New Jersey* was about to pass under the Astoria Bridge—this time without any distractions. As her long bow pointed once more toward the Pacific, her unmistakable lines turned into a hazy silhouette against the misty glare of the afternoon sun. It made a perfect image to remember the ship—heading out to sea and looking almost exactly as she had when built, generations ago.

Although my duty aboard *New Jersey* had been unofficial and could only be measured in days, I felt I too had been a part of the ship and in touch with a small piece of her history. But her career was over.

Upon return to Long Beach, the gloomy process of decommissioning would begin. In the post Cold War world of smaller defenses, the battleships' jobs seemed to be finished. While their demise has been foretold with every previous trip into mothballs, this time, it is a virtual certainty the Iowa-class ships will never steam again.

The USS *New Jersey* slipped across the bar and approached the horizon, turning slowly to a southerly course. Captain Hughes watched with twinkling eyes and a hint of smile creasing his lips, quietly taking in his last glimpse of The Battleship.

"Awesome," he murmured. "Just awesome..."

****

On February 8, 1991, the USS *New Jersey* was decommissioned for the fourth time in forty-four years, and it is now a floating museum in Camden, NJ. On January 16, 1992, Captain Donald E. Hughes made his last trip as a Columbia River Pilot and retired with over thirty-three years of service.

As of 2014, Dan Butler had been a dispatcher for the Columbia River Pilots for twenty-seven years. During his time off, he keeps busy volunteering on the Steamer Portland *in the engine room as fireman, and he serves as secretary for the Board of the Oregon Maritime Museum.*

Dan and his wife live on the slopes of Mt. Talbert in Clackamas, Oregon. They have three children. Dan enjoys photography—especially documenting ships, trains, and historic industrial sites—backpacking, hiking, and kayaking, has a passion for writing, and has completed a novel.

"Don't love nobody. Won't miss nobody.
The whole human race is worthless."

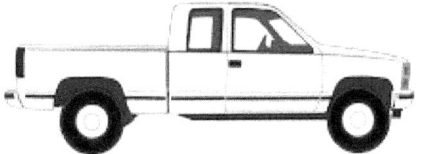

The Big Push

Oscar

"How many baking potatoes will you eat in two months—ten pounds worth?" Roger was making lists, organizing the household, and shaping me up in preparation for the two months he'd be gone upriver, purse seining for salmon for his job as National Marine Fisheries biologist.

"How many potatoes in ten pounds?" I asked.

"Probably too many if you don't bake any."

"Oh, I'll bake some—but I'll probably eat mainly new potatoes and carrots, and garden burgers. Are there any of them in the freezer?"

"A couple boxes." Turning his attention to our black and white charmer, Agness Rose, Roger said, "Yes, little cat. Jump up and I'll pet you. God knows you won't get much attention while I'm gone."

Little cat Agness weighed sixteen pounds.

"And not even a decent dinner, poor child," I commiserated with them both. "And no warm Bear chest to sleep on—life is going to be tough," I said as I patted my husband's chest.

"And remember, those dinky little bowls do not go on top of the soup bowls."

"Sure, dear," I said, grinning.

"Oh, hell, I might as well expect it. This place will be a wreck when I get back—the silverware all out of place in the drawer—every damn thing out of order in this whole house. Why can't you be systematic?"

"Like you? Only the gods are that organized. You leave tomorrow, April 3rd—so what day do you get back?"

"I'm leaving early in case the salmon run is early. If it's late, who knows when I'll get back."

"You're still planning to stay in Spokane?"

"No—Lewiston, Idaho, will probably be the closest base. In Lewiston, there are some motels with kitchenettes. I'll save quite a bit by cooking my own meals. How many more grapefruit should I get? They're only ten cents apiece this week."

"Are you taking some with you?"

"No, I've got too much gear to take along already. I'll buy supplies up there. I'll save money by not eating out—but I suppose you'll spend all I can possibly save while I'm gone."

"Of course. Agness, Coco, and I are planning to buy complete new outfits. And both the girls are hard to fit—tails, you know—probably have to buy custom made."

"I guess I'd better make out a list so you'll remember what I'm telling you. Don't forget to mail the taxes and write the check."

"One check will do for both state and federal?" I asked, innocently, picking up on his leaving off the plural. I liked to play the straight man when Bear got too bent out of shape. We usually called him Bear—for a lot of reasons.

"No, stupid, two checks. You don't need a stamp for the feds, but put one on the state's envelope. And don't forget to eat the leftover salad. Today's the last day before it goes entirely limp. You can put it on the cottage cheese, and don't forget to eat both cartons before they go bad."

I'd cut Bear's hair last night. He liked it cut every other week, but it would have to go until he got back from Lewiston in about two months—he'd never pay a barber. He'd taken a bath last night, too, and he'd gone to bed a little early. At 3:30 a.m., he was back downstairs gearing up for departure.

The boxes and bags he'd packed were by the door. His lunch was made. Two flashlights and a large knife sat by his jacket.

Roger continued on with his list for me. "There's a jam coupon from Safeway. They have blueberry and raspberry—the kinds you like. Eat the cooked meat in the icebox—both the roast and the sandwich beef. And there's three gallon of milk in the fridge—zero percent. It was on sale. Now look at the date when you get it out. Don't just grab like you usually do."

"My list says, 'Your car fueled and oil topped.' Does that mean it's to be done or you've already done it?" I asked.

"I've done it, and the oil was so low, it wasn't even registering."

There was no accompanying lecture, which wasn't surprising, as he'd been using my car as much as I the previous few months. I grinned to myself. In the past, he'd always sidestepped the blame and passed the guilt on to me, regardless. He really had improved—some.

"There's a couple dozen cans of cat food and forty pounds of Crunchies. I filled the big container, and there's another bag. If you run out—and you shouldn't—there's a coupon in the cupboard. And there's plenty of coon food—two big bags. Ration it so you don't run out—or too bad for them."

Bear knew I wouldn't let the raccoons starve. But, I wouldn't bother to come right out and say that I'd buy another bag if necessary. No point in borrowing trouble.

"Now, I've put clean sheets on and turned the mattress, and I shook the wool mattress pad and all the blankets. I've changed the cat boxes and dumped the wastebaskets. Think you can manage for two months alone by yourself with no one to do the thinking for you?"

"I doubt it," I said dryly. It wasn't that I didn't appreciate all the work Bear did around the house, but I couldn't help feeling like the slob half of *The Odd Couple*—the one who isn't Felix.

"Now, what's your address going to be?" I asked. "Where are you staying? What motel?"

"I'm not staying anywhere."

"Yes, you are. I saw the name of your motel in your notebook."

"What were you looking in my notebook for?"

"You showed me the date of *The Christian Science Monitor* article that had the cat book title in it. You don't want me to know because of the dancing girls?"

"I'm not taking the dancing girls—only the horse dog. And I may not stay in the motel you saw in my notebook, because our secretary said that area is noted for flea-bitten motels. I may want to change when I see this one."

"Well, call me as soon as you've decided and let me know your number."

"You don't need to know my number. I don't need no woman callin' me."

"Not me—it's Agness Rose. She may get lonesome. I don't know why you couldn't have told headquarters that you couldn't go because Agness will miss you."

"Maybe I thought about it—and maybe I didn't."

"At least you could stuff her in a duffle bag and take her along." To make my point, Agness obligingly came over and rubbed against Bear's ankles.

He picked her up and looked into her green eyes. "How'd you like to go along, Poop? Yeah, I bet you'd holler the whole way. We won't get in till eight or after tonight. That's sure to be a great day with you yellin' the entire trip. Sorry, Poop, you'll have to get along without me." He rubbed his chin on her head and put her down, regretfully. He really had a thing for that cat.

He made a cup of hot chocolate for each of us, and he ate a couple of sandwiches with his big mug full of cocoa. Finally, he was ready to go.

By that time, I'd taken my shower and stood in my nightgown for a last back scratch. "Now repeat after me. I love you and I'll miss you," I commanded.

"Don't love nobody. Won't miss nobody. The whole

human race is worthless." But he gave me a nice back scratch, kissed me, and said under his breath, "I love you and I'll miss you—maybe, especially if the horse dog runs off."

"What if the motel doesn't allow horse dogs?"

"They'll never see him—never even know he's there. Nobody sees the horse dog but me." He picked up his satchel of books, and I handed him his lunch sack.

Agness and I stood in the doorway as he started the company pickup. Our second cat, Jake, hid behind my car, waiting. Murphy, our third one, ran down the stairs and sat on the woodpile.

Bear got back out, scratched Murphy behind the ears, and said, "Goodbye, old man, take care."

Murphy purred contentedly.

Bear picked up Jake and hauled him back to the porch. He said, "The keys to my car are on the window sill, next to my chair. If you need to use it, try not to wreck it," and he turned back to his vehicle.

So much for a last hug.

He whistled for the horse dog, both doors slammed, the pickup started forward, and the taillights vanished down the hill.

"...my first lesson on love."

Like the Sea

Caitlyn M. Schmidt

I cuddled up in my mother's lap, and we rocked gently back and forth in the yellow light of lampshades and sunrays. I was four years old, and my world was brimming with questions.

A thick, twisting, fourteen-karat chain hung around my mother's neck, and a gold pendant rested just to the right of her heart. A plumeria and its leaves swirled around the barrel-shaped charm.

My mother rolled the barrel between her fingers, and I traced the lines of the handcrafted filigree with curious eyes.

"See the letters? *Kuuipo*. It means sweetheart." Dimples appeared in her cheeks as she read the black enamel-inscribed word on her Hawaiian Heirloom pendant. My mother wore it every day—my first lesson on love.

"Daddy got it for me on Valentine's Day in Hawaii," she said, rocking me in her gray and blue striped recliner. "That was back in the 1980s—before you were born, munchkin. Would you like to go there someday?"

"Yes, Mommy," I replied.

"Good. Daddy and I will take you soon. I think you'd love the Fern Grotto. It's a big, beautiful cave with long ferns growing on the ceiling. And we'll go to the beach every day so you can play in the waves and hunt for seashells. How does that sound, little love?"

Hawaii was the perfect destination for my mother. She had always loved the sea. She grew up visiting her family's oceanfront cabin in Cannon Beach, Oregon, and loved walking barefoot across the sand as the salty mist beaded coolly on her face. Even her name, Shelley, spoke to her affection for the tiny, white treasures that could be found dotting the beach. Her favorite was the scallop for its gently curved shape and radiating grooves, as if it were an open fan.

In 1986, my mother and father took time off work to enjoy a Hawaiian vacation and remove themselves from the daily bustle of teaching grade-schoolers and working in electrical engineering at Boeing. It was their escape from family, friends, coworkers, students, and the back-of-the-mind burden they carried—the absence of a child of their own after ten years of marriage.

My mother was a tall, long-legged beauty in her early thirties, her lovely smile contained between two crescent dimples and her eyes a brilliant, sparkling sea green. She had short, dark brown hair, cut in a style that curved around her head to rest at her neck and on her ears.

My parents held hands in cotton shirts covered with tropical flowers in full bloom and full saturation. Flower leis, shorts, and sandals completed their look, which could only be identified as "tourist," though they knew the islands well.

They strolled across the coarse Hawaiian sand as my mother looked for shells as namesakes and souvenirs. Rushing water was their soundtrack. While she cherished the few days they had alone together in the lush paradise, my mother longed for a tiny hand to hold as she traversed the beach—a little one with eyes like the sea.

On Kauai, my parents toured the Fern Grotto. Located along the Wailua River, the majestic lava rock cave, formed millions of years ago, was a natural amphitheater adorned by hundreds of hanging ferns rooted on and around the wide, gently curved roof.

My mother was filled with wonder. Tropical flowers grew in the foreground, and she heard the trickle of water in the background as droplets dripped down the fern fronds and danced on the cavern floor. It was the ideal romantic setting and had been a classic site for weddings since the 1960s.

After visitors were given a moment to explore, the tour guide called for the crowd's attention. "Welcome to the majestic Fern Grotto!" He gave a brief history of the site, noting its significance to the ancient Hawaiian royalty, then asked, "Do we have any newlyweds here today?"

A few couples raised their hands and were appropriately congratulated with applause, oohs, and ahs. My mother squeezed my father's hand, recalling their Hawaii honeymoon in 1976.

"That's wonderful," affirmed the guide. "How about ten year anniversaries?"

My parents raised their hands, shared a kiss, and then clapped for the others who had also achieved a decade of marriage.

"Twenty? Twenty-five?"

Each milestone was acknowledged, all the way up to sixty, before the tour guide asked, "Now, who here thinks they've been married the longest?"

The crowd chuckled. A few couples spoke up, each announcing their number with pride.

"Congratulations! Now, we'd like to celebrate the lovebirds here today with the Hawaiian Wedding Song," said the guide, and the tour's entertainment began.

My mother soaked the music into her soul as she watched the performers on a platform neighboring the formation's mouth. Ukulele strings were plucked, grass skirts rustled over bare thighs, feet stamped, hands clapped, vocal chords quivered, and rounded sounds escaped open mouths. The melody, sung first in the Hawaiian language and then in English, echoed under the grotto's sheltering dome and steeped in the damp air.

My mother whispered, "I love you," to my father as they stood in awe, arm in arm inside the song-soaked cavern. Contemplating the large, empty space, she could not help but associate it with the hole yet to be filled in her heart.

I would not appear in my mother and father's lives for six more years. But, once I was old enough, they took me to the ancient site. Finally, my mother shared with her little girl a place that had captured her heart. Finally, her daughter got to see the dazzling grotto with her own sea-blue eyes.

Caitlyn M. Schmidt was born and raised in the Seattle, Washington area. She graduated with a degree in English with an Emphasis on Creative Writing from Western Washington University.

Caitlyn has travelled to six continents via family vacations and college study abroad trips, and she loves experiencing new cultures and historic sites. She was married in 2016, and she and her husband celebrated their first anniversary in Hawaii—including a visit to the Fern Grotto. She is also the author of the travel guide, Fun Down Under: Australia & New Zealand.

"...they were nice clean goats—
as far as goats go."

The Day of the Back Porch Pie

Patricia Guerin

Aunt Dinah Stover, who lived just down the hill from us all the time I was growing up, was noted for her cooking, but not for her persnicketiness. She had a large dining table, but it was pretty full, what with the egg grading, the account books, maybe an extra brooder of baby chicks, all the catalogs she'd saved from years back, and her husband's collection of harnesses he planned to mend next winter, if he got around to it.

There was a direct route always kept open to the crank telephone on the far dining room wall. Her handy husband, whom she referred to as Mr. Stover to others, and Thee'door to his face—most others referred to him as just plain Stover—had invented a silencer so that the receiver could be picked up on the party line, and no one else would be the wiser. Since Aunt Dinah got no social calls of her own, she did enjoy rubbering in.

I believe the only time we heard of the dining room table being clean and used was when nephew Dwight David Eisenhower—whose mother was a Stover—came to call. I think he was a major then. He wasn't wearing his uniform anyway, this being a social call and all. I don't think Mamie was with him, fortunately.

Aside from being Dwight David's uncle—and before marrying Agnes, which was really her name, and settling in Oregon—Theodore had romped with another Theodore up Cuba's San Juan Hill and had many a high tale of adventure to tell. Also, he smelled quite high of goats, as he, like his wife, didn't think too much of bathing. The short, bandy-legged Theodore—who did also boast a handlebar moustache and spectacles, an exact match for Teddy R's—was a relentless inventor. He contrived a traveling mailbox, which would slide down the steep slope on a cable between their house and the Roseburg highway one hundred feet below. Aunt Dinah would crank it back up after the mailman's morning visits.

Another innovation was Theodore's use of a culvert installed by the highway department to accommodate the creek, which churned down off our Guerin ranch on the hill above throughout the winter. During the summer, the creek trickled beneath the feet of Stover's cows, going to or from the pasture on the other side of the highway, through the culvert. He carpentered a draw gate to discourage his cows and goats from swimming through when the creek was high and the pasture was flooded by the Coquille River.

All these conveniences—including a battery dynamo to run the chicken brooders on the back porch before the rest of us along that loop of the Coquille, east of Myrtle Point, were wired for electricity in 1939—were especially handy for Aunt Dinah, who could keep all her little chickens under the electric brooders on her back porch nice and warm. The goats, Billy, Rosie, and Tillie, slept there on cold nights and enjoyed the warmth too, which was all right as they were nice clean goats—as far as goats go. That was also the porch where Aunt Dinah churned her butter and that she used for serving up when she had a hay crew. In our rural Coos County area of Oregon, all the neighbors pitched in to help whoever was haying.

Theodore had made life so easy, several afternoons each week saw the Stovers on their way to town in their old Model A to sell the eggs and watch the action on the streets of Myrtle Point—population over 2,000, counting the rural residents. Aunt Dinah sat erectly steering, hands stiff on the wheel, knot of gray hair slipping loose to one side. She peered through her silver-rimmed spectacles, narrowly missing all strangers. She never came close to a local—all of whom pulled out on a shoulder upon recognizing her.

Anyway, as I said, if you weren't too religious about sanitation, Aunt Dinah was a great cook and went all out cooking for Stover's hay crew. The crew, of course, ate in the cramped kitchen less than an arm's length from the stifling hot wood stove. She usually selected my dad—"Laurrrinnn," she always dragged it out, letting his name roll over her tongue after it had rasped from her throat—to help with the servin' up of the pie. He wasn't too sure of the honor as he kicked his way round the this and that left over from the chickens and the goats on the loose and flapping linoleum floor of the porch. Aunt Dinah didn't hold much with mopping or with sweeping either.

This particular time—the time Dad always spoke of as The Day of the Back Porch Pie—he had served the first two pieces and was returning for the next set. He came through the door in time to see Aunt Dinah leaning over in her low-necked blue gingham gown. My mother once said that despite her ample girth, Aunt Dinah had the neck and collarbone of a turkey. But my dad said that she had a pretty neat ankle, considering the rest of her. I don't know how anyone could tell, because she always wore black lace-up, high-above-the-ankle shoes, which almost met the hem of her long dress.

Now the reason Aunt Dinah had her feet planted far apart and was bending over so low, was to retrieve a piece of pumpkin pie that had fallen on the floor. I don't mean to imply there was anything wrong with that porch floor, except that you might remember Aunt Dinah wasn't much for mopping, and the goats weren't much for sanitary practices. Luckily, the pie had landed bottom side down, and Aunt Dinah just slipped a spatula under it, neat as you please, and was depositing it back on its plate.

"There, Laurrrinnn," she said, in great good humor.

"Nothin's lost." She handed him the floored slice—which was only a little hunkered into its crust—along with another piece.

Dad didn't wear glasses, but he had better eyesight than Aunt Dinah, and he kind of lost his taste for a second piece of pie before he'd had his first, he always told later. The talking and laughing of the hay crew was steaming through the door at him, mixed with the smell of Thee'door, who was sitting one chair over from Dad's crony, Red Woods. Red and his missus—whose floor was so clean the dog was privileged to eat off it, according to Red—lived on Sky Ranch just up over the hill from the Guerins' thousand-acre holdings.

Red was just boiling out a hunting story where he made out he was the one who shot both deer, so Dad—the best shot around by far—would have one to tag. Everybody knew Red's eyesight was almost on a par with Aunt Dinah's. He was a practical joker and first-rate liar. Red had stolen many a march on Dad, and he needed a set down in the worst way.

Stover and Red were next in serving succession, and Dad's right hand held the slice of hunkered-down pie. Dad approached the table, started to serve the pie as it was, wavered, and at the last moment, crossed his hands, giving the glory of the porch floor pie to Stover.

Red's bacon was saved at the last second. But, Dad decided he still owed Red. So when Stover sent the men—old Mr. Bradley, Pomp Endicott, Red, and Dad—on ahead down to the field with the horses pulling the empty hay wagon, Dad had his chance.

"You know, Red, that pie you had at dinner..."

"Yeah, Lorin, Aunt Dinah can really set up a feed. And that second piece was about as good as the first."

"Not quite, Red, not quite. I don't think it could've had the same amount of flavor, 'cause the first piece was the one Aunt Dinah scraped off her back porch floor."

That's all it took. Knowing full well the condition of the back porch floor—and having a very squeamish stomach according to his missus—Red barely made it beyond the next haystack. He looked green the rest of the day. From then on, "The Tale of the Back Porch Pie"—his ultimate triumph over Red—became Dad's favorite story, telling it one way one time and the other way the next, much to Red's eternal despair.

The next summer, when I was ten, I got to work in Thee'dore's strawberry patch several mornings a week—for twenty-five cents a long row! One slack day, Thee'dore told me I could help Mrs. Stover in her pantry. The pantry was a tiny lean-to doglegged from the hired-hand dining area. It had a real sink with both hot and cold water—thanks to Thee'dore's plumbing ingenuity—and a small rope from which hung several sacks of almost-completed cottage cheese. I'm sure you know there is sour cream involved in the process, and the lean-to with its one window tightly sealed—reeked.

My stomach voted with Red Wood's and could barely stay afloat those several hours of washing encrusted bottle and jar. Especially since the small drain board could have used a good scrubbing, and the floor was almost on a par with the back porch. And when it was time to leave, I had the grace to murmur, "No thank you," to the shiny dime Aunt Dinah offered me, while adding that Mama said she would need me at home from then on.

Patricia Guerin was born in Paso Robles on the way to Los Angeles, California, for her father's new job on the aqueduct. When the Great Depression hit, he lost his job, and the family moved to a logging and farming town in southern Oregon. She was first in her class at Myrtle Point High School, and while attending Oregon State College, Pat worked on the school paper. After graduating, she taught at Taft High School in Lincoln City for a year, and then while raising three children, as a school librarian all around Oregon. Nowadays, officially retired, Pat likes to "mess with plants," read, and help people improve their reading skills. She lives in Astoria, on the Oregon coast, with her husband and a few cats.

"Did somebody steal our clothes?"

Swim Caps, Goggles, and No Leaves

Ben Hamar

"I'll give you both a dollar if we turn around," said Napoleon as the car crossed the bridge to Sauvie's Island, Oregon. "C'mon. A dollar apiece if we quit right now. It's sooooo cold and I'm sooooo out of shape."

Napoleon lied. He was in great shape—he'd ridden an overloaded mountain bike the three thousand miles from his home in Nome, Alaska, to Portland, Oregon, in a single month. Napoleon was six feet of hard-charging, high-speed, low-drag, iron-ass cyclist. He was also a lousy swimmer.

It was a cloudy, late-October day. Napoleon and his friends, Clemson and Conrad, were driving to the nudist beach at Sauvie's Island—ten miles down the Columbia River from Portland. They intended to go for a swim—to Washington and back.

"I wish I'd stayed on my bike and kept riding south." Napoleon had stopped in Portland to visit his alma mater, Reed College. He'd looked up his former roommates—Conrad, a fellow graduate, and Clemson, a senior at Reed.

"What does not kill you makes you stronger," Conrad pontificated. Rad had spent the summer at the Fort Benning Infantry Officer's Basic Course, trying to figure out why the army called people who carried everything they own on their backs "light" infantry. "Maybe the guy who said that is a dead mad man."

"Maybe you shouldn't quote Nietzsche to a philosophy major."

"If it's too cold, we can always get out." Clem tried to restore harmony.

Clem never got angry—but he always got even. Rad and Napoleon had snuck into his bedroom early that morning and beaten him awake with pillows. They wondered just what form payback would take when it came.

The car left the hard-surface road and bumped along the final half-mile of gravel that led to the nudist beach. Clem, Napoleon, and Rad got out and walked through the woods that separated the road from the beach. They stood watching the river flow silently by, the same color as the clouds that covered all but a sliver of the sun.

The three stripped down.

"You're not going to wear those shorts, are you?" Napoleon snarled, pointing at the swim trunks Rad wore.

Rad *had* hoped to do exactly that. "Of course not! When you do something insane, why do it half-way?" He pulled them off.

Clem steeled himself and dove in. He stroked toward deep water while Napoleon and Rad recoiled from dipping their loins into the numbing liquid.

Clem quickly returned. "Let's not do this. Washington is half-a-mile away, and the water is just too cold. This isn't smart."

The group teetered on the brink of falling into the abyss of rationality.

Rad was seized by a realization. Napoleon might whip Rad in all things athletic, and Clem, "Mr. Hey, Ladies," might flirt with chicks Rad was scared to look at, but *I'll be the alpha male, the big dog, if I go first!* "Whasssamatter? Forget your personal products?" His blood toxic with testosterone, Rad plunged forward and took off for Washington.

"S**t!" Napoleon yelped. He shook his fists in the air and dove in.

Clem shrugged, then followed. He settled into a regular stroke. His body warmed to the work slowly—until a grinding noise intruded upon his awareness. "Napoleon!" He grabbed Napoleon's arm and pointed.

"Rad!"

A massive ship loomed downstream. A Japanese flag fluttered from its stern. "TOYOTA" was painted on its hull in letters telephone pole tall.

"A car carrier!"

"We forgot to look both ways before we crossed."

"If we don't want to be hamburgered, we'll have to stay here until it passes."

"I don't wanna be the largest chunk of meat ever ground in mid-stream."

Treading water in the middle of an ice-cold river is a poor survival technique. Clem, the tallest and thinnest of the three, realized this first.

"Guys, I can't feel my fingers anymore." He turned back toward Oregon.

Rad and Napoleon watched him go. They realized safety demanded they stay together but were reluctant to abandon the trip.

"Let's do it!" Napoleon was pumped. He could see the Washington beach clearly as the car carrier's wake lifted him several feet up, shook him violently, and dropped him back. "Don't think. Act!"

The two resumed swimming. Rad gradually pulled ahead. Looking back, he noticed Napoleon's fingers were splaying apart. He was slowing. Rad switched to the breaststroke and fell in behind the Alaskan.

On the Washington side of the river, a current waited. Rad swam to the beach as quickly as he could. Napoleon made shore a quarter-mile farther downriver. They ran toward each other, bobbing and weaving in the loose sand as their oxygen-starved bodies kept trying to make swimming motions.

"We should've worn trunks. I think my dick fell off

while we were waiting for the ship to pass!" Rad flapped his hands together.

"Man, remember the time Bryan dared us to swim the river at daybreak? Remember the cold wind blowing and how Bryan had to throw sand and threaten to beat you with a stick to make you swim?"

"Yeah. And I remember 'Mr. Alaska' standing right next to me, too!"

"Well, you better go find a big-ass log to wave at me 'cause I don't want to get back in." Napoleon was serious. His lips were blue, his jaws were chattering, and he hugged himself while doing a little dance to stay warm.

A smile curled Rad's lips. "Can I have your bike if you don't make it back?"

"Screw you, a**hole!" Napoleon grabbed a handful of sand and threw it at his friend.

They moved into the tree line to escape the wind. Someone had built a lean-to there and hung a plastic shower curtain over its front. Napoleon wrapped the curtain around himself. He sat down in the sand.

"Clem was right. We should've turned around."

On the Oregon shore, Clem hadn't seen Napoleon or Rad emerge. Over an hour had elapsed since the three had parted. If Rad and Napoleon were alive, they must be unwilling to attempt the return swim. Since the Washington shore was a roadless wildlife refuge, Rad and Napoleon were stranded.

Clem gathered together all of their clothes and carried them to the car. He drove down the road until he came to a marina with a grocery store.

Inside, half a dozen unemployed townies sat around drinking coffee. Calmly, so as to not make a scene, Clem asked the clerk if he could make a call to the Coast Guard.

"My friends swam across the Columbia. They're stuck on the Washington side."

Every head in the building turned as he spoke into the phone.

The Coast Guard officer on the other end of the line

questioned Clem closely.

"What were the two individuals wearing?"

"Ummmmm..." Clem paused. "Swim caps and goggles."

"I mean what clothes were they wearing?"

Clem held his breath for a second. "They were nude."

The pair in question was sitting on their buttocks in the cold sand.

"Napoleon, we gotta do it! We're not going to get any warmer, and there aren't any ships coming."

"Stinking river!" Napoleon's Nome-trained survival instincts took over. He jumped up, ran down the beach screaming, and dove in.

Rad, shocked, watched Napoleon's back recede. He faced the same cold plunge and was suddenly hesitant. No witty quotes from Nietzsche came to mind.

Shame drove him in. Hyper-competitiveness made him strain to catch Napoleon. By mid-river, the two were even.

"We're going to make it, man! The next time we get out, we don't have to get back in again." Napoleon felt great.

"Attitude check," Rad shouted back.

"Aiiieee-athabascan!" they both screamed.

Rad exuberantly switched to the butterfly and slammed through the final few body lengths to shore. "Let's run!"

They yawed and swerved up the beach, giddy after the long, cold swim. It felt wonderful to move freely, unimpeded by the water.

Pounding along, feet sinking deep in the oily sand, Rad and Napoleon enjoyed every step of the mile upstream to where Clem and the clothes would be waiting.

When they arrived, Rad was confused. "Where are our clothes? Did somebody steal our clothes?" He ran in a circle, waving his arms. "Did Clem drown on the way back? Maybe he decided we couldn't make it and went to get help."

To Napoleon, the answer was clear. "That dirt-bag took everything, and he's sitting in the car laughing at us!"

They walked along the soft-dirt trail to where Rad had parked the car. It was gone. A long moment of silence followed as they stood absolutely still. A cool wind blew over their nude bodies. Rain clouds filled the sky.

"The sun is only an hour from setting. We're half a mile of gravel road away from a hard-surface road that's twenty-five miles from home—and we don't have any clothes." Napoleon's voice was very cold, very hard, very Alaskan. Then it changed. He smiled. "This is hilarious, Rad! We're gonna have to walk down this road barefoot! Let's not think about it, let's just do it." He slapped his hands together and strode off down the middle of the road, stoically ignoring the sharp rocks.

Rad sighed and followed, keeping to the road's dirt shoulder and picking his way around the blackberry vines that reached out aggressively. "Clem. You die. I kill you." Rad sighed again.

They expected to find Clem on the other side of every curve. He was never there. They expected to find him at the end of the gravel, laughing at their sore feet. He wasn't there. Clem was playing the ultimate practical joke on them, the kind of joke people laugh at for years.

The first car they met actually accelerated as it went by. The woman driver wanted nothing to do with two naked, crazy people. But the second one, a green pickup with a gun rack, pulled to a screeching halt. Its driver jumped out holding the mike to a citizen's band radio. "Did you two just swim across *that* river?" he yelled, waving at the Columbia as if it mattered which river they'd swum across.

"This is surreal, man," Rad muttered.

"I've found them. They're okay. Call off the Coasties." The driver spoke into his C.B. The words hardly left his mouth before he had to dive for the side of the road as two more pickups and a familiar car drove up.

"You're all right!" Clem shouted happily.

His friends glared at him. Clem hastily began pitching them their clothes. The occupants of the pickups all stood around with big grins. They seemed a little disappointed the fun was ending, though.

"Thanks, guys." Clem waved his arms broadly and smiled. "Thanks for everything." The locals trailed off to their trucks.

"We're sorry we're still alive," Rad hissed ungratefully as the onlookers revved their engines and reversed direction.

One of the drivers leaned out his window. "Next time, bring a fig leaf!"

Rad and Napoleon piled into the car, letting Clem drive and explain at the same time. But not for long.

"You called the Coast Guard! You did this to us 'cause we beat you awake this morning, didn't you?" Rad pounded the back of the driver's seat.

"Why take our clothes? Did you think my next-of-kin would want my jock strap and tennis shoes to remember me by?" Napoleon punched Clem's arm.

Clem, who had had only the best of intentions, warmed to the idea of himself as the villain. He leaned back in his seat, adjusted his sunglasses, and grinned. "What can I say, guys? Except—I wonder if that reporter I talked to will spell your names correctly."

"...the old Dodge looks like a remake from *Grapes of Wrath*..."

Three Dollar Hammer

Norm Maxwell

It's Monday morning, and Dennis and I are waiting in the darkness by the tree cooler—the refrigerated container for the seedlings—on Seneca Street in Eugene, Oregon, waiting for our crew to show up. A dozen vans and crew cab pickups come and go, taking hundreds of thousands of trees out to the unit while we cool our heels. The old Coast Range Resource Area has over one hundred acres—burned in last summer's Siuslaw Fire—that need planting now. It will be a long, exciting week hanging out with our Hispanic tree planting crew.

Finally, a battered white Dodge crew cab shows up, and Ramón and half a dozen planters from Salem, Oregon, pile out. We huddle and decide how many trees to take to our first unit. The men form a human chain and hand a mix of 6,000 Douglas fir, red cedar, hemlock, and incense cedar in paper bags and waxed cardboard boxes to Ramón as he stacks them in the back of the rig.

I pull the cord that shuts the doors to the cooler as Noi, the lead man, ties a tattered reflective tarp over the load, and we head west out of Eugene for the thirty-one acre unit.

The pavement ends, and, in the dawn's early light, the old Dodge looks like a remake from *Grapes of Wrath*, crowded with seven people and the full load of trees. The ragged tarp flaps in the breeze. Dennis is driving our lead BLM pickup, and it rapidly pulls ahead on the grade. We wait at intersections until the crew catches up. Finally, we pull up on the dead end of the landing.

The crew jumps out to survey their new unit.

"Culo Diablo," Enrique dubs the steep and deep burnt canyon "we" are about to plant.

Now comes the unspoken question as to what sort of inspectors Dennis and I are. Will we be "landing lizards" and sit in the pickup on the landing? Or the kind who follow a crew and make sure no shortcuts are taken?

I put on my calf-high, White-brand cork boots as the crew fills a tub with water from five-gallon plastic blitz cans to dip the tree roots in. This makes them heavier to carry, so an inspector watches this process like a hawk. I instruct the crew to load the bags they wear around their waists with mostly fir, but to take a handful of hemlock. One man will plant mostly red cedar in the creek bottom. The hardier incense cedar will be planted on the western aspect slopes where they will hopefully survive the long, hot days of summer.

The planters hoist their heavy tree bags high onto their waists and cinch them down while shouldering paper bags filled with 120 dipped trees and trudge down a scorched ridge to the bottom of Culo Diablo. I tote two bags of dipped trees tied to my shovel like a suitcase and half a bag around my waist in a borrowed tree bag. This gets the crew's attention. Most inspectors are unwilling to play pack mule. Dennis carries trees too.

We stop about fifty horizontal yards above the creek, and the crew sets down its paper bags of dipped trees. We can see now that there is enough water in the creek to dip trees in for the next run.

Antonio takes the lead and plunges his planting shovel into the ground with his foot and rocks it back and forth until the soil breaks. Then he slips a vibrant, green fir seedling into the hole and stamps the earth closed. Octavio picks a spot ten feet away and does the same. I assume the position as El Cid del Stumpo—the Stump Lord—on a blackened old-growth stump, leaning on my shovel.

The planters plant in a loose formation, moving to the lowest corner of the unit before Ramon hollers, "Pa'tras!" *(Take it back!)* and everybody reverses and moves back on their line.

I start digging trees to make sure the roots were planted correctly. When I'm through inspecting, I replant the tree so it's deep in the ground and pointing straight up. The planters can tell that I've done this a few times. When they reach their paper bags, they carefully remove the dripping trees and pack them in their tree bags. They pack the ones Dennis and I toted too. I am still wearing my half bag. Next, they all plant one line up the steep slope to the rigs far, far above. The February sun comes over the big trees to the south as I burn the used paper bags in a pile on bare ground.

We miscalculated—the crew runs out of trees before reaching the road, and we all deadhead the last seventy yards back to the rigs. The crew drags out the traditional propane ring, warms up pans of beans and rice and such, and rolls them up in tortillas. Dennis and I sit in the rig, eat cold sandwiches, and read the local paper. In a few minutes, Ramón cracks the whip, and the planters pour more water in the container and dip more trees. Tomorrow, we will pack dry bags down to the creek and start there.

Anyone who hasn't abused himself with commercial tree planting can't possibly understand the effort it takes a crew to plant many big trees on rugged terrain. The heavy tree bag cuts into your waist, and your hands become engrained with dirt. The pay is lousy with all the cutthroat competition for planting contracts.

If you have landing-lizard inspectors, you can skip ground and space the trees a little wider—but that isn't the case here. The only thing the crew has going for it is that it isn't raining.

Oops, here comes the rain. The crew loads up again, and we descend the ridge, sliding on the fresh glaze of mud.

I find a poorly planted tree and holler, "Inspector no

es contento!" My limited Spanish can cover any tree-planting situation.

Antonio is eighteen years old and a master planter. He senses where there is rock and drives his shovel into dirt every time. While he is planting one tree, he is looking ten feet away where he will plant the next. He is almost twice as fast as the rest of the crew. I time him, and he plants a tree every ten seconds on the steep slope. I make it a habit to give him the trees I pack when he runs low.

The thirty-one acre unit we are planting had been covered with twelve- to fifteen-foot tall firs from a previous plantation after logging. The fire wasted them, but we can see the earlier fir planting hadn't survived everywhere on the harsh west-aspect slopes. I am hoping the incense cedar will.

The planters sing Mexican country western songs and clink and clank amongst the wet rocks. Dennis is new at tree planting inspection, but it isn't rocket science. The most important thing for an inspector is to be there. If the inspector doesn't care, there is no reason anybody else should.

I tell Ramón the old joke: I buy hammer handles for two dollars and hammer heads for two dollars and assemble them into complete hammers and sell them for three dollars—and you know what? It beats planting trees.

Ramón doesn't get it. Oh well.

The crew is planting exactly like I want now, so I fall in behind and plant a few trees with my fire fighting shovel. I bang the blade on a handy stump when it muds up. The crew hasn't seen an inspector plant very often. This will be something to tell their friends.

If the planters don't plant all the trees, they will have to drive back to the cooler and return the extras. This will make their long day even longer. They are working close to the top now, and I carry trees to Antonio, the tree-planting machine.

"No mas pinos!" somebody hollers, and they all

troop to the crummie—their beat up truck—on the landing, throw their tools in the back, and collapse on the seats. Ramón will drive the long trip back to Salem.

"Six at the cooler—mañana," I tell him.

"Sí," he answers.

Tomorrow we will work the far side of the canyon Diablo.

Norm Maxwell worked for the Bureau of Land Management and was a wild land firefighter in the summers. He rides a BSA motorcycle. If he could possibly be right, he has never been known to back down. He is not popular among paper shufflers. The authors of the stories Swim Caps... *and* Three Dollar Hammer *are brothers.*

"Police, firemen, and others were standing there staring up at the damage."

The South Tower Slid North

Mike Donovan

It was a warm, sunny Tuesday, the eleventh of September, 2001, more summer than autumn in New York City, and I was having my last cup of coffee before heading out for a job interview in lower Manhattan. I lived on Myrtle Avenue in a neighborhood called Fort Greene, which was just north of the downtown Brooklyn area.

My wife, Mary, left for work early in order to attend a Labor Board hearing at the Javits Federal Building, also in lower Manhattan. I thought she was going to a labor arbitration, which would put her in the midtown area a number of blocks from the World Trade Center.

The local jazz station announced a plane had hit one of the World Trade Center towers. There was no sense of urgency in the announcer's voice, so I thought, as did many others, a small plane flying off course had struck one of the towers. I turned on the TV and saw a second plane hitting the South Tower.

I left for my interview. I thought the fires in the towers would soon burn themselves out and things would go on pretty much as usual. I walked to Fort Greene Park, which offers a good view of Lower Manhattan. I could plainly see the towers smoking and burning. The wind was blowing the smoke southward toward Staten Island. A few people had gathered on the hill to watch, but it was pretty quiet.

Shortly, I headed up Myrtle to catch the F Train at the Jay Street Subway Station, which was nearest my apartment. The F Train headed west to the lower East Side of Manhattan. The A and the C trains had stops at the World Trade Center (WTC) at Chambers Street.

When I got to my stop, the C Train was sitting in the station, and the announcer said it would be routed over the F Train line, which would take it around the tower area. It would get back to its 8th Avenue route at West 4th Street where I could get out and walk to my interview.

I got on the C, the doors closed, and the train pulled out of the station, not along the F Line, but along its regular route, which would take it to the Trade Towers. I thought the situation must be somewhat in hand if they were going to move trains through the WTC station, so I stayed on—intending to get out at West 4th.

There was only one more stop for the C train in Brooklyn before it reached Manhattan, so it was a very short time before the train pulled into the Broadway-Nassau station just to the west of the WTC. Rather than proceeding, the train just sat in the station, and I thought the likelihood of getting through the WTC was probably slim. I left the C train in order to catch one of the uptown East Side trains, which could be caught just a few blocks away near City Hall. It would also give me a chance to see, up close, the damage to the WTC buildings.

I exited on Fulton St., which ended at the WTC complex. I could see the entire North Tower from the top almost to the bottom, blocked out by a three or four story building housing a Borders Bookstore. I walked as far east as I could. This put me at the corner of Broadway and Fulton Street across from St. Paul's Church.

While there, I ran into a rabbi friend of mine, Michael Feinberg, the head of the New York Labor Religion Coalition. His office was in Lower Manhattan, and he had been on the scene from the beginning. He had seen the planes hit the buildings, people jumping from windows, and all the horrors of being that close. He was totally shaken up.

I don't know exactly what time it was then, but we both stood staring up at the North Tower. The top thirty to forty floors of the South Tower were also visible to us from that perspective, but the flame and smoke in the North Tower was what I was looking at between bits of conversation with Michael.

Police, firemen, and others were standing there staring up at the damage. There was no sense of urgency to move. We were but one block from the WTC complex. Most people were moving out of that area, so I was as close as I could get without being inside the cordoned-off area.

We were only there a short time when I saw the top of the South Tower sliding to the north—to my right. I shouted to Michael, "It's coming down!"

We both started running down Fulton Street toward the South Street Seaport. People were screaming and falling down in panic as they tried to escape. I headed down Fulton Street to the subway station from which I had just come.

It still looked like the South Tower was tipping over. The realization that it had been collapsing in on itself didn't dawn on me for a couple of hours after that. No one knew what to expect. I kept thinking I had to get away from the falling facade, air conditioning units, and whatever else was coming our way.

As I reached the subway exit, passengers were coming up the stairway. They had seen people running but did not know why. I told them that one of the World Trade Center buildings had fallen down, and they should go back down to protect themselves from whatever may be falling into the area. Then I turned around and saw a wall of white smoke rolling slowly down Fulton Street right toward me.

As I got to the bottom of the subway stairs, a great cry came up from the platform where my train was still sitting. I assumed the smoke had gone through the subway tunnel and had reached the platform below.

I ran back out of the subway and saw a deli a couple of steps from the stop. People were pushing into the store to avoid the coming smoke, which was getting thicker and thicker. It was evident that as more people came in, the more the store was filling with smoke.

Before it got too bad, I left the store and headed toward the South Street Seaport a couple of blocks away. Suddenly, I was totally engulfed in a white powdery smoke, smelling like burning plastic. The smoke was so thick, everything went white. I could see no cars, no buildings, no people—only this white powder that was everywhere.

I made it to the corner past the Strand Bookstore and headed north away from the smoke. It wasn't until I reached the Brooklyn Bridge underpass that I was able to look back and assess the situation. There was no South Tower!—only the North Tower still aflame and spewing black smoke.

The police were trying to get people out of the area. I'm a big walker in NYC, so I know how to get around. I was totally covered in white dust but made no attempt to clean myself off.

I headed north—planning to get to my old job rather than getting back on the Brooklyn Bridge and walking home. I walked up through Chinatown and Little Italy without looking back. When I reached the corner of Bleecker and Broadway, a couple of blocks north of Canal, I heard people screaming. The North Tower had just fallen!

It was then I turned around to look at New York's new Lower Manhattan skyline. It looked strange without the World Trade Center towers, though I had always considered them pretty ugly.

A young woman took my picture all covered with the white dust. I must have been a mess.

When I got to my workplace, I found my wife was frantically trying to get in touch with me—she suspected

I had gone to the WTC out of curiosity, which was only partly correct.

She told me she had come out of the WTC stop on the subway shortly before the first plane had hit. She had been standing outside the Federal Building waiting for her witness who would testify at the National Labor Relations Board.

The Federal Building was about ten blocks north of the WTC. She and a Federal Security officer were standing on Broadway when they both saw the first plane flying low, down West Broadway.

Surprised, they looked at each other, and he commented, "That plane looks awfully low." Then they saw it fly straight into the North Tower.

Mary still decided to wait for her witness, but the officer had no doubt about what had just happened, and he quickly moved to the building to begin securing the area. When her witness arrived, she told Mary she had been coming out of the subway station when the first plane hit, and she had been terribly freaked out by it all. She and Mary headed back to midtown. They ended up walking up West Broadway and saw the second plane hit as they headed north.

It was an experience neither Mary nor I will ever forget.

"Navigating became increasingly more
difficult as the sun went down..."

Northeast by Northwest:
An Expedition into
the Heart of Maine

Marcus Handy

As dusk was falling, we flew down the snow-bordered highway toward the mountain lodge at eighty miles per hour in Susan's Pathfinder SUV. From behind the wheel, she spotted something ahead, about ten yards off the road—a large bull grazing. Fear instantly overtook her.

She accelerated and started swerving and muttering, "Oh my God, oh my God."

Attempting to put more distance between the moose and us, she drifted into the oncoming lane. Ahead—only a quarter mile out—I saw an eighteen-wheeler coming toward us. The large truck started blowing its horn, and we continued to close at a combined speed of 140 mph. Susan had lost it! Although her mind was as fragile as a house of cards right then, I figured the truck was worth mentioning.

"Susan, there's a truck..." I whispered—like a cool breeze on a hot day, so as not to disturb the cards—and pointed forward.

"Oh my God—the moose!" she screamed.

I clutched the handle above the window in a death grip and braced myself for my imminent and illogical demise. Who in their right mind would choose a forty-ton truck speeding toward you at sixty miles per hour over a 1,400 pound, stationary moose?

Well, we passed the moose and got back in our lane, with a full two seconds to spare, narrowly escaping ending our short lives as human pancakes. All the while, the moose just stood there, chomping on its mouthful of winter grass, blithely watching the foolish human spectacle. Seth—following behind us in his truck— pulled over and stopped to photograph the moose. He got a prize-winning shot of its posterior as the stoic creature finally got scared and ran off.

We finally made it to the mountain lodge, alive, and checked into our cabin to find it well stocked by our friends. Our group included Susan, Brad, Brendan, Don, Josh, Matt, Stacy, Seth, Tom, and myself. They had enough beer to go around, and I supervised preparation of my Aunt Marian's lasagna recipe for dinner while Don established the rules for our vacation.

"Rule number one: no talk about work!"

After dinner, we visited the lodge and its bar, shot the breeze, played air hockey, and played a weird game where you toss a ring on a hook—must be a New England thing.

Suddenly, a coverall-wearing telephone man burst in through the door exclaiming he'd just hit a moose. Translating his thick Mainer dialect was a challenge, but it sounded like he'd been in the same spot where we'd almost died earlier—claiming to have hit a "laaarge bool moose."

I knew it was a little presumptuous to hold the man's moose responsible for our near-death experience. Who knew if the two moose were one and the same? Especially considering the behavior of the moose in the two timely-but-separate instances was quite distinct.

Did it really make sense that the same creature that chose not to run in front of the SUV, then fled from a parked truck and a 150-pound guy with a camera, had then decided to go head-to-head with a utility van? Preposterous!

I didn't buy the telephone guy's story, and I took

another sip of the bitter house microbrew and went back to getting beaten at air hockey. Seth decided to go outside to verify the man's claim. He returned with a handful of moose hair, so I had to go out and see for myself.

The large Dodge van had a smashed windshield, crushed bumper and left front-quarter panel, a big dent in the side—presumably where the moose had bounced off—and was covered in tufts of moose hair. Apparently, hitting a moose is no joke. But, I'd rather hit a moose than an eighteen-wheeler—any day.

Just before 10:00 a.m. the next morning, our little group was all bundled up for the cold winter weather, and we set off on an expedition to Moosehead Lake, sixty miles away. We rented motorized sleds and rode out in a single file. Our group's most experienced rider and designated guide, Big Don, led the way. At 6' 7" and 270 pounds, Don was not the kind of guy you could ignore. But, he was an engineer—not a navigator.

Anyway, it was good Don took the lead to keep us—mostly me—rookies from going too fast and getting hurt. Even so, I decided to "test the limits" of my vehicle, crashing three times in the first half of the trip. It wasn't just that I went too fast, but that the reaction distance needed between yourself and other sleds was a lot different from driving a car. It really depended on the ability of those ahead of you controlling their own sleds.

The first three crashes weren't too bad. The sled didn't roll over. I just got thrown off at twenty miles per hour or so. Thank God for soft snow, my helmet, and an understanding of the concept of how to fall.

I got really irritated with Susan, who also crashed, and travelled the slowest of anyone in the party. All day long, she kept saying I "sucked" at driving. I say it takes a lot of work to hide your own insecurities. Perhaps the incident of the moose and the eighteen-ton truck still rankled her a bit.

We got up to Moosehead Lake around noon and stopped at a gas station to top off the sled tanks. Three of our group members decided not to refuel, leaving some doubt as to when they would run out of gas.

After gassing up, we went for lunch at the Green Toad Restaurant. The place would've been my pop's favorite restaurant if he'd lived in Greenville, Maine. He'd always referred to people he didn't like as toads—and the place just had his style.

We traversed over and parked our sleds on the lake itself. I didn't realize it was a lake until I drove between a gated pair of red and green buoys frozen into the ice. I changed out of my wet socks into a dry pair and dried my wet pair on a heater in the restaurant. Not exactly the most posh manners, I admit, but the Green Toad's policy seemed to favor helping its patrons combat frostbite.

After lunch, our expedition headed out to visit a 1964 B-52 Bomber crash site in the nearby mountains. We kicked our sleds into high gear to see just how fast they would go and found that the engines were governed down to a top speed of sixty miles per hour. Don claimed his could top out at 120 mph, but he didn't feel like showing off. The little vehicles were fast and fun, but also loud and constantly belching smelly exhaust.

On the way to the B-52 wreckage, I was thrown from my sled twice—that took me to five crashes—because others in the party decided to stop suddenly, too short a distance ahead of me. Following everyone else wasn't exactly my favorite sport.

We reached the plane crash site about forty minutes later. There was a plaque with details about the victims and the one, lone survivor.

Apparently, the plane crash killed a lieutenant colonel, three majors, two captains, and two lieutenants. The tech-sergeant had been the only one with enough sense to try to eject, but his chute failed to open, as he was too close to the ground. His ejection seat, with him still in it, landed upright in the snow, and amazingly, he only broke his foot. The sergeant had to tough it out in sub-zero temperatures for the entire night before he could be rescued.

Though we only spent about twenty minutes at the B-52, our time was at a premium. It had taken us almost four hours to make it to the crash site. That included ten mini-stops of three to five minutes each for the lunch break, and to count noses and make sure no one had been left behind. The sleds were due back at the lodge by 4:00 p.m., or we'd be charged $25 per hour for each late sled. That put the pressure on our "guide" to lead us back the sixty-mile route faster, and with fewer stops.

We were all depending on, and implicitly trusting, our guide. If I'd thought about it, I might have taken more of an interest in our route. But early on, I'd just been trying to keep from being thrown from my sled.

For the sake of emergency contingencies, I'd taken along some extra water, which froze, a small flashlight, which I must have lost during one of my crashes, and a pocket knife. I'd had a sneaking suspicion I might need the knife, but it turned out I didn't.

The three of us who hadn't fueled up did so, before we headed back to Greenville. I decided to fuel up again, too. Better safe than sorry.

We jumped on the Interconnected Trail System (ITS), Rt 85 South, and really flew along. We made great time, averaging forty miles per hour.

Although the ITS system was well-groomed and mapped, it was poorly marked and downright confusing. Every five miles or so—unless they forgot to put one up, or you didn't see it—there'd be a tiny paper sign stapled to a tree saying you were on the right track. Every mile or so, you'd see a sign with a black arrow on a yellow background telling you that you were on track—but which track? The signs were made of cheap paper, which dissolved in the elements and undoubtedly fell off the trees. The routes were confusing—on the map, ITS 87 and 85 merged, and so did ITS 87, and 86, and 89.

On the last segment of our return leg, the trail was infrequently marked ITS 87, while the map said ITS 86, and later ITS 89. So which was it? Consequently, about an hour after, we'd obviously missed our turn. We stopped to check our position. Don's portable GPS—which, because of the cold, hadn't worked earlier—was fully operational, having warmed inside his thermals for the previous half hour.

Only Don could read it, but it showed we were approximately at the same latitude as the lodge—about twenty miles too far east. Don and Tom, who always had all the answers, talked about it and figured the turn onto ITS 87 had to be coming up soon. So, we kept on going.

By dusk, we'd found a promising trailhead near Breakneck Ridge. We also spied what looked like a real mountain man there. The guy had a long beard and wore leather clothes with wool stitched into them. His boogers were frozen in long strings of ice on his mustache. He was piling his sled dogs into the cabin of his snowplow-equipped, half-ton pickup truck when Don and I approached him for directions. He brought out a map and pointed to where we were. We asked him about the trailhead, and he said he didn't know where the trails were, but they should be well-groomed.

Basically, he didn't tell us anything useful, which made me doubt he was a legitimate mountain man. It's widely known that *legit* mountain men have impressive knowledge of their local area. Regardless, the map, GPS, and mountain man all concurred. What we needed to do was, "Go West!" How simple. We were decidedly comforted.

We regrouped the sleds and pushed on, stopping to consult the map from time to time at different forks in the new trail. To our dismay, it wasn't a trail going straight west as a road would be expected to. Navigating became increasingly more difficult as the sun went down, and we were cold, impatient, and hungry.

We had three different maps, and the best one had been torn in half by two over-eager members of the "navigation staff," which had grown to include Tom, Seth, Brendan, and myself.

I knew we were lost when Brendan said, "Show me where this Breakneck Ridge is on the map."

I looked at it, turned it right side up, and informed him, "It's on the other half of the map. Who has it?"

Twice, Don and Seth decided to override me, so we went left when I had said to go right. I felt a warm touch of pride when the GPS showed we were getting farther from the lodge—but I didn't feel better for long. After all, we were getting farther away from hot food and warm lodging.

We mucked about in the woods for another good two hours. Eventually, we intersected a real road, followed it on the ice alongside the road, found a house, and stopped to ask directions to where we could get gas. I was one of four of us who weren't running on fumes. We got lost again on the trail to the gas station, but thankfully, finally found it.

We took time to thaw out in the Quickie-Mart attached to the gas station. The locals coming in shook their heads and sighed at the sight of a bunch of greenhorns. The lady attendant got a bit upset with us because we took over all six gas pumps with our sleds, stood around inside the store warming up, clogged access to the counter, and bought fuel, candy bars, and liquids in increments. I gassed up *again*, just to be cautious.

We eventually left the store and returned to the wilderness—wandering ever closer to the lodge. We stopped after an hour and forty-five minutes, confused, because no one had seen the sign for the lodge. My brain's wheels began turning.

One of the disapproving locals at the Quickie-Mart had mentioned we had a good hour and a half to reach the lodge from the gas station. I calculated the time for the five stops we'd made and rounded up my estimated average stop time to five minutes each. That put us at ten minutes from the junction, and just like magic, it appeared on the left, ten minutes down the road. There, we turned onto the final eight-mile leg and headed toward the lodge.

I flipped my headlights on bright, jammed my

throttle forward, and took over the lead. I went so fast, no one could keep up with me.

It felt good to be free, no longer constrained by slower riders. It was safer for me, too. Six miles down the road, I stopped and waited for three minutes until everyone caught up. I took off in the lead again, and soon there were no headlights on my back. I gunned it on the straightaways and slowed before the turns. I swerved and shifted my weight to maneuver the sled expertly to keep on track and avoid trees and rocks.

With only one mile to go, I came to a long straightaway and gunned it to fifty miles per hour, slowing to forty-five as the trail inclined into a fairly steep hill. As I crested the hill, the trail turned to the left. I conservatively negotiated the first half of the left-hand turn at a reasonable thirty miles per hour and accelerated to forty-five miles per hour through the second half of the turn, which took me to the outside of the road.

While still in the turn, I could see the trail ahead dove into a steady decline for about fifty yards and then banked sharply to the right. I'd learned from my previous crashes that if I tried to brake during a turn, especially at that speed, I would surely topple the sled.

I let off the gas completely and shifted my weight to the left to try to maneuver the sled. I began to turn, but the ass end of my sled was drifting toward the outside. The right rear quarter of my runner caught something, and the sled stopped dead and rolled to the right. I was pitched into the air and flew in slow motion twenty or thirty feet before crashing into the brush. I hit pretty hard and got shaken up, but I was A-okay.

Laughing out loud, I surveyed the damage to my sled. The left-side mirror was missing, there was a broken light and a cracked cowling, and the windshield had popped off. Maybe I'd missed my calling as a Hollywood stunt man. I really enjoyed my crash. Although, after the fact, I'm not sure I enjoyed crashing the sled as much as I would have enjoyed spending the

$900 it took to repair it elsewhere.

Riders and sleds started appearing as I got up from the wreck. Seth and Don told me they'd seen my wrecked sled and a log on the ground they'd figured was my dead body. I think maybe it was that stinking log that tripped up my sled!

Seth ran up and asked, "Are you okay, man? How many fingers?"

I walked away with no concussion and no broken limbs—not even a headache or a bruise.

Psalm 91:11-12 says, "For He will give His angels charge of you to guard you in all your ways. On their hands, they will bear you up lest you dash your foot against a stone." I'm grateful those angels weren't asleep on guard duty.

To re-cap our grand adventure in snowy, winter Maine—we encountered a large, potentially hostile creature, navigated a vast and unforgiving wilderness, survived sub-freezing temperatures, and weathered our own incompetence. It forced clarity of thought in a fluid and rapidly changing situation. It served as a reminder to us—people who were perhaps a little too used to the protective blanket of civilization—by grounding us in a basic way, revealing our vulnerability to our proud, blind selves. It was a great experience, and I would recommend it to anyone.

Marcus Handy was born in Bellingham, Washington, in 1977. A graduate of the U.S. Coast Guard Academy in New London, Connecticut, he serves in the United States Coast Guard as a Lieutenant Junior Grade and is stationed in the Northwest. Marcus would describe himself as a thoughtful Christian man who loves challenge and adventure, feels at home in the beautiful wilderness of the Northwest, and is a seeker of a meaningful life.

"We were eager to sink into the culture."

The Year of the Horse—2002

compiled by Karen Kenyon

At 6:40 a.m. on an October morning at Portland International Airport, we herded each other onto a Beijing bound plane—five Astorians and one "honorary" Astorian—for a three-week tour of China with Odysseys Unlimited. Armed with personal talismans from the Chinese Zodiac—Carol Barth (Pig), Bobbi Brice (Buffalo), Portlander, Maggie Collins (Rabbit), "Bert" Levy (Dragon), and Karen Kenyon and Susi Brown (Tiger)—were ready for adventure.

We eagerly awaited the experience of a culture so different from our own, one in which years are named for animals and the society reflects a spiritual sphere.

Chinese tour groups wore red or yellow caps to identify them. Our American group did not. Can you imagine Americans donning yellow ball caps as part of a tour uniform?

But one of our guides, Ho Hong, identified himself with a Santa hat on a pole, saying we could easily find him in the crowd. "So, ho, ho, ho!"

Coughing and wheezing in the smog-laden air, we set out on our life-altering adventure. We moved easily to the front of lines at tourist places, getting first-rate service.

"We all have 'cousins,'" said our tour leader, Mike Zhao, hinting a conspiratorial smile. We immediately understood these "cousins" were well paid.

We were eager to sink into the culture, open our hearts to perhaps learn more about our own culture by experiencing another. That indeed turned out to be the case.

It seemed the Chinese live outside. The numerous parks were filled with people in action—tai chi, dancing, flying kites, stitching on silk, playing board games, "walking" their caged birds, and practicing calligraphy on the concrete, using buckets of water and huge brushes. Everywhere, people were playing music on stringed instruments, singing in shrill voices, not the mellow sounds of American acoustical guitars played by full-throated folk singers. It was all we could do not to plug our ears and run! Open hearts, yes. Open ears, well, maybe not.

Straightaway, we loved the dumplings and the beautifully presented chrysanthemum fish. We tried the snake wine—yes, a real snake in the bottom of the bottle. But, our American eyes, minds, and stomachs couldn't quite deal with the "chickie paws," pig hands, tongue, stewed goose lungs, duck intestines, and duck web feet. Some parts of another culture maybe don't need to be sampled. We could learn just by watching.

In Beijing, we realized we were at a thoroughly Western hotel when we had to ask for chopsticks at the dinner table. Mike was very cautious about what we ate—no unpeeled fruit, no uncooked vegetables. We could have only bottled beverages or local beer.

Sometimes, he walked around lifting plates from our tables. "You can't have this."

We wailed in protest to no avail. We were hungry for fresh lettuce salads.

The city of Fengdu was half torn down and looked inefficient and disorderly. We smelled diesel fumes, sewerage, and cement dust. Produce stands provided color: grapefruit, bananas, green beans, bok choy, onions, and leeks.

We got there in time to see the Yangtze River, the Three Gorges, and the stunning cliffs and valleys before the Chinese government destroyed so much beauty in order to build the enormous Three Gorges Dam.

Sometimes overwhelmed by sadness, we saw the precious historic sites, which would soon disappear under the harnessed water. White flags on the hillsides marked the level to which the river would rise. We knew too well the impact on fish and the environment of damming a thundering river.

Many of the Chinese adopted a motto of, "You like tradition from us; we like modern from you." They, of course, wanted modern conveniences. That kind of life demanded the electric power the dam would provide.

Mike also repeated, "In China, people rule people. In America, law rules people." In China, there is no Environmental Protection Agency.

> *During this part of the boat trip, when I stop to stare at the cold, green waters, and the eternal rock walls, I feel a sadness that this wondrous beauty, the harmony of water and stone, should be covered over soon, not to be appreciated by human eyes and hearts...the rub of water against stone for geologic time, and the dance of molecules that render water from stone; this should be celebrated. While there are other magic places like this gorge (Ba Gorge), I'm sad that humans demand its disappearance.*

—Maggie's journal, 10/19/02

At the tourist entrance to the dam site, security was tight. Our driver had to leave his driver's license with the guard, who had counted heads. He could not retrieve his license until we returned to the gate and the guard had certified we were all on board.

The country was well on its way to modernization, but much of the work was being done by well-muscled young men who carried cement blocks hanging from bamboo poles across their shoulders. Many were barefoot, shirtless, and wearing cotton shorts and hardhats. They were dismantling the cities to be inundated by the dam, removing everything that might interfere with the movement of the river traffic.

Except where large projects were under construction, we didn't see the bulldozers, heavy trucks, and huge jack hammers that are at every American building site. We were amazed daily at the mix of the ancient and modern.

The Chinese national bird is the crane, the long-legged, long-necked, incredibly beautiful dancing bird. But, our guides joked, it is also a building crane, a common sight where the high-rise apartment buildings were under construction.

The Chinese first called steam locomotives "iron dragons," trucks "iron oxen," and bicycles "steel horses." Early Chinese roads were just wide enough for two horses.

Everywhere in China, streets were filled, literally, with a rich mix of pedestrians, bicyclists, cattle, old trucks, donkeys, and water buffalo pulling carts, all weaving around autos and buses. Carol called it the "City Traffic Ballet." It was a rhythmic movement of goods and people, seemingly flowing without effort— very different from American rush-hour traffic. Bobbi's impression echoed her fellow travelers' sentiments.

As I turned to enter the pathway leading to our next destination, I was immediately paralyzed. Taller than most of the people in this part of China, I looked out over a sea of black, bobbing heads, as hundreds of Chinese walked up the hill toward the temple. Though I was sure it was obvious I wanted to join them on the walkway, no one stopped to let me in. Not wanting to be the rude American, forcing my way in, I waited my turn...looking at the passing faces...hoping for some sign when it was my turn to enter. Nothing! Eventually, seeing the rest of my party moved ahead, I gingerly stepped onto the pathway. I was astonished! The flow gently embraced me and carried me with it. There were no dirty looks. No one grumbled because I had cut in front of them. No one even bumped into me!

I left China feeling the Chinese are a very wise people. On occasion, when facing a challenge, I have called on the memory of my experience with entering the pathway. It reminds me I don't need to compete. I don't need to wait for answers. I don't need to fear the outcome. All I need do is step into the flow.

Instead of scientific naming at the Reed Flute Cave, we viewed "Birds in Singing Fragrant Forest." What Westerners see as fine stone carvings can be viewed by Chinese as statues of evil spirits. Human observations on either side of the globe seem to underscore the yin and yang of life.

In Xian we were awed by the ranks and ranks of soldiers sculpted to guard an emperor's tomb. Every face was different from the others, as in real life, every costume detailed and life-like, each figure only a little smaller than life-size.

The soldiers were made of vitrified terra cotta, fired at temperatures between 1,235 and 1,700 degrees Fahrenheit, which created a natural glaze from the chemistry of the clay, making it immune to disintegration. They were created beginning in 246 B.C.

Jade Dragon Snow Mountain, in the foothills of the Himalayan Mountains, was a breathtaking sight, as was the bus ride up a narrow, serpentine road overlooking beautiful vistas. Gondolas transported us to the top of the mountain where it was quiet and serenely beautiful. The few hardy souls who lived there were welcoming but unconcerned by visitors. We felt a spiritual calmness and connection with nature.

But at the entrance to every historical site, no matter how sacred, a flock of peddlers flanked our path.

"Hello! Hello! T-shirts, one dollah!"

"Boo yah," we learned to say—"No want"—as we stepped around them...usually.

We loved watching the monkeys play. And the villages were indeed rich with corn. Bushels and bushels of ears were drying on the roofs, providing a sort of insulation between two layers of roofing, spilling out over the edges—a feast for the eyes, as well as for the monkeys and the people.

On the riverboat trip on the Li River, perhaps the most romantic adventure of our journey, the river boatmen had no radar, no radios, no huge motors. They signaled from the prows of the boats, controlling river traffic themselves. Boats showing red flags like showing stop signs took the right of way. Those holding white flags waited. They pushed the vessels along with long bamboo poles, the poles working in concert with the boats' small motors—both were necessary.

The classy ship we were scheduled to take on the Yangtze River was in dry dock, so we were put aboard a vessel of much less grandeur. It was a training boat where Chinese men were housed on one side, we tourists on the other.

Because of this, all were inconvenienced—the workingmen having to double up on lodging and the Odyssey group adapting to the change. Some of the other members of our tour were furious, threatening a lawsuit, grumbling about this insult, letting it get in the way of their enjoyment and ours, not willing to see it as part of our Chinese adventure.

Our little party laughed as the ship swayed during mealtime, our bowls and chairs sliding from side to side.

Carol quipped, "Hey, girlfriends, let's share! Eat whatever comes your way."

The grumblers forgot to behave like guests, not owners, of the host country. Our little entourage, however, made the best of it all, giggling our way through Yangtze waves of nausea and splendor.

Karen had a special fascination with the Chinese plumbing, as well as the animals, bicycles, laborers, and signs. We smiled at, and enjoyed, the signs and didn't feel at all superior about their amusing phrasing of English. After all, we spoke only a couple of words of Chinese.

"Star-rated toilet ****"

"This way leads foreign guests out only."

"The Path of Love: For the aged, for the sick, for the disabled, for those in urgency, emergency passengers, please wait here."

"The giant panda has 'appetite for sweats, like sugar...'"

Accustomed to huge tractors and combines on American farms, we were awed by the picturesque hand-laboring in the fields around Jingshou, a "market town" of seven million people. Clusters of farm structures punctuated miles of varied-size farm plots, very well tended. Scattered ponds were used to raise freshwater fish—we had some for lunch. This was a green-tan quilt of hugely productive farmland. The farmers called their rice crops "four stoops" from planting to harvesting, which they do twice a year. Allen, one of our guides, said food was China's number one priority.

In a similar way, accustomed to huge ships, noisy work vessels, fast sport boats, and an occasional elegant motorized sailboat on our home river, we were plunged into thoughtful comparisons between the Li River and the Columbia River. The fishermen in some places still used cormorants as their "fishing poles."

Our "dirty half dozen" embraced China with our eyes, ears, hearts, and imaginations—renewing, strengthening old, and building new friendships. Travel does that.

Though many years have passed, and some of the sharper images have begun to fade, our enthusiasm for sharing memories of this special time with one another remains as strong as it was on that autumn daybreak at the airport so many years ago.

"What I saw will be stamped
in my memory forever."

Somewhere
in Germany

Bill

Dear Mom,   April 16, 1945

Today has been our first beautiful day for some time. Sure is wonderful to lie out in the warm sun. My truck is in Ordinance, so until it comes back, I won't have too much to do.

Have a great amount of laundry to do but find it hard to get started. These days find me awful lazy.

Received Maida's box of March 1st today. Glad to get everything. I do advise not sending talcum powder in a paper container again. Both times they were busted and all over everything. Ah, yes! I'm smoking a cigar right now.

The package and three issues of the G.I. are all the mail I've received for ten or more days. Can understand the reason, so don't think I'm complaining. We're just moving too much for it to catch up.

I saw something today that every man, woman, and child should see, if only in a newsreel. I visited one of Hitler's concentration camps we overran the day before we pulled in here. Even after seeing the horrors of such a place, I find it hard to grasp that it is true.

The area of the camp covers about ten acres. Into this area were crammed sixty to seventy thousand people, some German political prisoners, but most of the people from countries Hitler had occupied. It is a place of filth, starvation, and disease. You can't imagine the number of men that slept in one building, just piled on top of one another in bunks four rows high.

There were 20,000 still in the camp, and a great percentage didn't even look human—skin stretched over bones. When you enter the place, several former prisoners who speak English are anxious to show you around. They want you to know what really happened.

One large building was used for the ones that were nearly dead. In this place they lay until it was all over, then they were loaded on wagons and hauled to an incinerator where the bodies were burned in a systematic manner. I saw skeletons, and partly burned bodies, still in the ovens. Outside were piles of bodies waiting their turn—stacked just like so much cord wood. In another corner is a pile of ashes, those of over four hundred people!

Then there is the place where they were hung, not to die fast, but so as to suffer horribly. Our guide told us of the beatings and many hundreds of murders he had seen the S. S. men do. In fact, the policy of the camp seemed to be that of working the people until they were worn out and then let them starve to death.

They worked from four in the morning until eight at night, many times much longer. The guide also said that every day many died, and dead lay around the area all the time. He estimated that between ninety and a hundred thousand died or were killed in this one camp.

I saw the hospital and operating room where legs and arms were cut off without the use of anesthesia. Today I watched doctors work on some of the patients that are so bad. There isn't enough flesh left to even look human. You've probably seen pictures of people in Greece starving—well that's what all these look like.

If you came into the camp with gold teeth in your head, about two weeks is all you lived. They killed them just to get the gold fillings.

The guide, a prisoner from the camp, also said that

the camp commander's wife looked the men over, and the ones with the best skin were killed, and handbags and lampshades made from it.

Maybe you're wondering why I'm writing all this— I'm doing it because it is the most horrible and inhuman thing that anyone can imagine. The world should know so as to get a better idea of this kind of people we are up against.

People in the town four miles away when they were questioned said they didn't know anything about this place, that they didn't do it, so why should they be to blame. Every last one of them couldn't keep from knowing what was going on. They are the ones that backed such a devilish scheme of world domination— the Super Race! Ask the ones who were prisoners there. They know!

Official photographs and records have been made of all this. I just hope the world as a whole gets to know about it. This is just one of many such places.

Over the gateway is a sentence in German. It says, "Right or wrong, my Fatherland!" Another over the ovens in the crematory, I've nearly forgotten, but it's something like this, "The worms and rot that torment my flesh are gone now—I love the fire and the light, burn me but don't bury me."

What I saw will be stamped in my memory forever. It's something you can't erase.

Must write a few more tonight, so here's hoping to hear from you real soon. Am sending another box with a sword and knife, also other things I may pick up.

Hello to Dad and Maida.

Love your son,
Bill

Editor's note: I acquired a copy of this handwritten letter while teaching 5th and 6th graders back in the 1980s. I found it so poignant, and as it told of a piece of WWII history, I kept it all these years.

Like Bill said, it is something "every man, woman, and child" should be aware of, and it should never be forgotten.

A note written on the letter by his mother says Bill was with Patton's army, and the concentration camp he wrote of was Buchenwald, near Weimar, Germany. Buchenwald was established in 1937, was one of the first and the largest concentration camps on German soil, and its remains are now a permanent exhibition and museum.

"The furry omnivore was down
on all fours, looking right at me."

Little Bear

Dan Heiner

The valley I live in has three mountains surrounding it. As you look east, Green Mountain is on the left, at 2,200 feet high, and to the right is Sister Green, at 2,000 feet. Saddle Mountain is due east about five miles away. They all have logging roads around them, and Green and Sister Green have roads to the top. Saddle has a state park with a trail to the summit at 3,200 feet.

My ten-mile run that memorable morning in early July 2003 took me up and around on the Green Mountain road. The sun was shining, the sky was blue, and the air was cool, crisp, and filled with the scent of evergreen trees. It was a beautiful day in the Northwest.

About six miles into my run, there was a five-way intersection at the top of the hill. Any way I went from there, it was downhill all the way back home. I usually stopped to rest at this intersection.

On that day, I decided to skip the rest and started on down the hill. I came around the first corner, and about twenty yards ahead of me was a black bear in the middle of the road. I stopped dead in my tracks and stood *very* still. My body went into fight or flight mode—every muscle tensed, every nerve ignited, and all of my senses heightened.

The furry omnivore was down on all fours, looking right at me. I didn't know who was more scared—the bear or me!

Black bears have long claws for tree climbing, and

like other bears, very large teeth and powerful jaws. I think both of us were nervous and unsure of what to do next.

He whoofed at me—three times.

I began to form a plan of defense. I slowly stooped down and picked up the two biggest rocks I could find and held them behind my back. I thought, *If he charges, at least I'll get one good hit on him.*

The bear lumbered to the side of the road and whoofed at me back over his shoulder a few more times. Then, after whoofing one last time, he bailed over the bank and ran off into the brush.

When I could no longer hear him crashing through the woods anymore, I started my run again and continued down the road—but I kept the rocks in my hands, just in case.

Since that day, I've always called that intersection "Little Bear."

"It didn't take him long
to come up with the perfect way
for us to nearly kill ourselves."

The Magic of Rock Climbing

Jerel "Supe" Lillywhite

Climbing stories told around the campfire tend to dwell not on disasters in the Himalayas or the 2014 avalanche on Mount Everest that killed scores, but rather on the victories and failures of those telling the tales. It is in these stories the real magic of climbing is found. To truly understand the joy of the journey, you must either experience it yourself or hear it straight from the climber as he relives his own epic adventure.

Like most of my truly great and miserable climbing trips, the adventure that stands out most vividly in my climbing experience was shared with my climbing mentor and best friend, JJ Cieslevicz.

Those who know JJ understand this quiet, moody man was not meant for modern society. While cell phones, computers, and ATVs completely perplex and/or anger him, other older technologies and practices like using a sewing machine to make his own pants, doing complex math in his head, and living off fish he catches with his bare hands come completely naturally to him.

Women love JJ for his chiseled features and rustic style of dress, but it's a rare female indeed who appreciates his lifestyle or his ideas of romance. A lovely evening for JJ has nothing to do with expensive dinners at fancy restaurants with violins playing softly in the background. Rather, JJ believes women are best seduced by sitting around a smoky campfire while cans of chili and tortillas on a forked stick cook over flames.

JJ and I have had many adventures together, including daring first descents of unnamed slot canyons, three consecutive failed attempts at summiting Mount Nebo during the winter, and living for twelve months in matching '95 Toyota Forerunners—his gold and mine green—as we worked on our college degrees. It is safe to say that on all of these adventures—while the ideas may have been mine—the driving force, expertise, and cursed persistence keeping us going all flowed from JJ.

The most vivid adventure I remember started in June or July in Saint George, Utah, the most heavenly place on earth—if you don't mind the heat. Summer days get well into the hundreds and have been known to reach over 115 degrees.

I had recently returned to Saint George from working in Trujillo, Peru—appropriately called "the city of eternal spring." Every day, year round, the low temperature is sixty-two degrees and the high is seventy-two. But, stupid as I was, I called up JJ and told him I was ready for a real adventure in the Saint George heat. It didn't take him long to come up with the perfect way for us to nearly kill ourselves.

Early in the morning, we traveled to Utah's Snow Canyon State Park. The park, while only ten minutes outside of town, is a virtual climbing paradise with 500-foot sandstone walls rising from the sandy floors below. True to form, JJ had chosen a style of climbing I was absolutely worthless at. Known as "traditional climbing," the style requires the climber to jam his hands, feet, and sometimes his entire body into cracks in the wall and slowly inch his way upwards in order to ascend. Nevertheless, JJ started up, and I foolishly followed.

As we slowly made our way up the vertical face, it became clear that we were not following an established route. Established routes typically have fixed anchors to belay your partner off, i.e., control the rope in case your partner falls, and are cleared of loose rock, sand, plants, insects, and spiders.

JJ happily informed me we were not on such a sissy route but were instead climbing in a "desert alpine" fashion, which really meant, "climbing up a piece of crumbling sandstone and knocking rocks down on top of each other."

When climbing a route as tall as the one we were on, climbers don't ascend it all in one go. First of all, their ropes aren't long enough, and even if they were, lifting the weight of the rope after the lead climber has ascended 100 feet would be extremely difficult. Instead, the lead climber climbs up about 100 feet, belayed from below by his partner, clips into or builds an anchor, and belays his partner up to his position. The process then repeats over and over again until they reach the top.

On our adventure, JJ was the lead climber and I, the follower. I watched him ascend section after section with ease and then had the pleasure of trying to repeat what I had just seen him do. The whole process reinforced my long held belief, "JJ is not human."

In places where he simply floated along, I found myself sweating, swearing, and doing anything I could to find purchase on the sandy, crumbly rock. Rather than using just my hands and feet to grip the rock, as climbers typically do, I was employing every spare inch of skin I had—and suffering accordingly.

To make the experience even more unforgettable, there seemed to be an abundance of sand, sticks, bugs, and spiders, which kept falling in my eyes, in my hair, and down my shirt. When we met up at the top of each pitch, it looked like we'd been climbing entirely different routes.

About three-quarters of the way up our route, we began to be aware of how hot it was becoming and how little water we actually had with us. We had brought plenty of water but had left it securely stashed at the bottom of the route along with our packs and our hiking shoes. That, it turned out, was what led to the real adventure of the day.

At about 1:00 p.m., we finally reached the summit. Despite the pain and misery of the climb up, the view that spread out below us was spectacular—Utah's entire Snow Canyon State Park in all its majesty. Light brown sand dunes and blue sage bottlebrush lined the floor of the canyon. The canyon walls were a layered tapestry of color: dark reds and browns at the bottom, where the iron content in the sandstone was greatest, lighter pinks and reds in the midsection, and flawless cream-colored sandstone at the top. In some places, hard, black basalt capped the sandstone cliffs, the remnants of where ancient lava had flowed over the once-buried sandstone.

Above that, perfect blue skies stretched in all directions. In the distance sprawled snowcapped Pine Valley Mountain, towering above the surrounding landscape at 10,000 feet in elevation. As scratched up and worn out as I was, I couldn't help but appreciate the incredible view we'd earned from our climb.

As we sat there admiring our beautiful surroundings, we discussed how we were going to get down. Typically, this is accomplished by rappelling back down the route you just came up. But doing this on a route as tall as this one would require there to be fixed anchors along the route, or for us to abandon some of our precious climbing gear on the wall. Obviously, leaving anything costing more than about $5 was unacceptable to the two of us. Climbers are notoriously stingy when it comes to leaving gear behind, and JJ and I were no exception.

The only possibility left was to start the four-mile walk back to where our hiking shoes and water supply waited. If only it had been a straightforward hike, on a well-established trail, it might not have been so bad. Instead, those four miles consisted of scrambling down slick rock faces inclined at forty-five degrees or more, and after that, a long, torturous slog through a sandy wash. Our feet were on fire! The only shoes we had to walk in were our climbing shoes.

Climbing shoes, if you've never worn them, are often

described as rubber-coated, extremely tight ballet slippers. Ours fit this description too well. Mine were at least two sizes smaller than my normal size ten, and JJ's were, if possible, even smaller. While they were bearable to wear for seventy-five feet of climbing at a time—and necessary for the thin footholds we stood on—trying to walk four miles across burning hot sand and rock in them was pure misery.

As painful as it was to keep walking on our burning feet, the thirst plaguing us was much worse. If you've never been desperately thirsty, let me describe it for you. It goes beyond your lips cracking and starting to bleed. It goes beyond your tongue swelling in your mouth and feeling like a hot, dusty piece of sandpaper. It even goes beyond the pounding headache you develop as your water-deprived brain begs you for liquid. The worst part is your complete lack of strength and vitality. You want to walk forward, to put one foot in front of the other, but doing so is so hard!

"Walk," you say to your feet.

"Water!" they shout back. "Give us water, and we'll walk!"

This battle is repeated on every step, every long, long step, until you find water or simply give up.

I vividly remember thinking how funny yet tragic it would be if we young, avid climbers, who had traveled over much of the Western United States in search of adventure, were to die within sight of the hills surrounding our homes. But our lack of planning on the matter of bringing proper footwear, and adequate water for a day as hot as this one, made it seem a real possibility.

As it turned out, a fetid pool of water saved us! Just when we thought we were too hot to go on, we found the pool, and nearby, a small cave. As desperate as we were for water, we still couldn't drink from the filthy pool. Instead, we bathed as much of our bodies in its shallow depths as we could to cool down. While we huddled in the shade of the cave, JJ took off his shirt and tore it into thin strips we used to fashion sandals. We rested for half an hour, then, much cooler, though still piercingly thirsty, we started out again.

Renewed from our brief rest, and shod with what felt like the cushiest footwear in the world after our long walk in our climbing shoes, we finally arrived back at our packs. In minutes, we drank the gallon of water in JJ's pack, and we were still thirsty.

Wearing our hiking shoes again, and with water back in our bodies, we looked up at our climb one last time before we headed back to the car. Somehow, the 400-plus feet of climbing didn't seem so bad. As for the hiking, well, I doubt either of us will ever forget shoes or water again.

I say "again" because we both knew as we took our first steps back toward the car that even though the trip had been long, miserable, and hard, hidden in the suffering, we had experienced what few people do these days—the rush and struggle of the climb, the unparalleled feeling of victory, the awe at the top, and the battle to make it back home.

Aided only by the gear on our backs, the skill in our hands, feet, and heads, and our reliance on each other, we had conquered the mountain. Thirsty or not, perfectly prepared or not, we'd be back on the wall soon.

Jerel "Supe" Lillywhite's parents instilled a love of the outdoors in him and his seven siblings at very young ages. Most of Supe's growing up years were spent in the red hills behind his house, building rock forts and playing in the red dirt of St. George, Utah.

He met JJ in 8th grade, and their friendship grew as they shared stories of hiking and camping. Both have worked as professional climbing guides.

Supe graduated with a Bachelor's degree in History from Utah State University, and he was married in 2014.

"...these men were talking about throwing me in jail!"

Welcome to Romania

Stephen W. Houghtaling

Some people may think that spending all day in Paris would be exciting. It would seem so, unless, of course, that entire day was spent confined to the Air France waiting area in the Charles de Gaulle International Airport, because that's what happens when you miss your connecting flight.

I booked my trip several months in advance to travel from Portland, Oregon, to Bucharest, Romania, to retrieve my college-age daughter, Lindsey, who had been working in the orphanages in the city of Iasi. She had been there four months. I was excited about the prospect of picking her up, having her show me where she had worked and what she had done, doing a little sightseeing, and then returning home just before Christmas, 2002.

Purchasing the tickets was satisfying. I had an accumulation of air miles saved up and was able to get Lindsey's coach ticket to Bucharest by spending air miles. Just for fun, I asked how many more miles it would cost for me to fly First Class to pick her up. Not having traveled internationally very often, and never First Class, the opportunity appealed to me. I was told that it would cost only a few miles more to make the trip First Class. So, I opted for it.

I spent the night prior to departure in a hotel close by Portland International Airport. To me, a trip is enjoyable three times. First, looking forward to it, then actually taking it, and a third time, as I review it in memory. Three trips for the price of one!

This one was to be particularly fulfilling, as Lindsey had been gone four months and we had missed her. Also, a different part of the world beckoned. Flying First Class—an added bonus!

Early in the morning, I was at the airport to catch my flight. I looked forward to walking into the First Class line to check my baggage, and to the much-anticipated question, "Where are you traveling today, sir?" and being able to answer, "Bucharest, Romania."

Sure enough, I walked up to the counter, the ticket tender asked me where I was going, and I replied with a big smile, "Bucharest, Romania."

She handed me my ticket in a First Class-lettered jacket, and I went to the First Class lounge to wait for my flight. I had been in such a lounge only once before. I enjoyed being there again. Food and beverages are available for free, as are plugs with which to recharge and use your laptop computer. The seats are leather. Exceedingly plush!

When departure time approached, I left the lounge and went to my gate. First Class passengers are invited to board first, and with an inside smile—one cannot appear to be a rookie when flying First Class—I produced my ticket and boarded the plane. I showed my ticket to the flight attendant and was seated in my first, First Class seat. Leather—and very comfortable. Even before I sat down, I was asked if I would like something to drink.

We flew non-stop from Portland to Atlanta. After a two-hour layover, I was to board a flight from Atlanta to Paris for a subsequent connecting flight to Bucharest. Lindsey would pick me up at the airport there. Then we would board a train for a seven-hour ride to the north to end the trip—finally arriving in the city of Iasi, Romania.

If I had been excited to board the plane in Portland and fly First Class to Atlanta, I was ten times more excited to fly First Class internationally. It was amazing in terms of service and room. I waited in the special lounge in Atlanta until time for departure—again boarding first. Upon entering the plane, I was shown to my international First Class seat.

The seat reclined to 160 degrees—almost flat. Footrests came out of the bottom of the chair. I was given a travel bag with eyewear to shield the light, earplugs to keep out the noise, and socks to keep my feet warm. Also included were toothpaste, mints, and lotion. Each seat had its own television screen. Fantastic! When I stretched my legs out as far as they would go and pointed my big toe as far forward as possible, I could barely touch the back of the seat in front of me. Unbelievable! Especially since I'm six-foot-four.

I had an amiable traveling companion, a pediatrician. He was flying to Paris and then on to a different part of the world. This was also his first opportunity to travel First Class internationally. He was appreciating it seemingly as much as I.

At dinner, we had a choice of appetizers and entrees. Served on china, the food was wonderful. When they brought the ice cream cart down the aisle, we selected sundaes, complete with toppings; choices of nuts, cherries, etc. Delicious!

First Class gives you an extra big, extra thick blanket and draw curtains to isolate your seat and to keep out the light. Sheer comfort! Also, multiple movies are available on your individual screen. Splendid!

The flight across the Atlantic was about nine hours—and that was when the trouble started. We left Atlanta about an hour late because of some unknown—to us—problem. The pilot assured us that he would try to make up the time—Standard Operating Procedure (SOP). In reality, they fly the plane at cruising speed, the optimal speed for fuel conservation with regard to the weather.

The delay was important because it meant that my making the connecting flight from Paris to Bucharest was in jeopardy. I thought it might still be possible to sprint through the airport, make it to my gate in time, and catch my plane. But, "No, no, it is not possible," everyone protested.

At the Paris airport, it's very difficult to get around. Delta doesn't have gate privileges. They must park on the tarmac. You take buses around to the terminal you want. Lines, lines, lines! All of a sudden, the fun of traveling First Class was swallowed up by the fact that I might miss my connection.

Might turned into did. In spite of my best efforts, there simply was no way to catch my connecting flight. Air France was kind enough to get us out on the next flight, but it would still arrive after 10:00 p.m.

It was about noon. That meant that Lindsey was sitting and waiting for me in the Bucharest airport, thinking that I would be on the flight I should have been on. I had no direct way to contact her. I called my wife, Lynne, back in Oregon to explain the problem and hoped that when I didn't get off the plane in Bucharest, Lindsey would also think to call her mom for help. This occurred.

Lynne informed Lindsey that I had missed my flight and that I would be arriving around midnight. This made Lindsey feel better emotionally, but not physically. What that meant was that she would have to stay in the Bucharest airport for another twelve hours. She had already been there waiting for fourteen, so it meant she would sit in the airport for a total of about twenty-six hours.

I realized, counting *my* travel time, that I would have been awake about thirty-six hours by the time I landed in Bucharest. Forced to wait, and wait, and wait in the Air France First Class lounge, my fatigue took over, and the enjoyment of the amenities faded.

I befriended a fellow traveler in the same predicament who was hand carrying some needed mechanical part to Bucharest. Finally, it came time for us to leave. The plane was packed with scheduled passengers, as well as those who had missed their plane. There were no empty seats—SOP.

The flight was uneventful. We arrived in Bucharest around midnight, and I had some difficulty retrieving my luggage. Finally successful, I was able to go through customs—no contraband—and then the door opened to the waiting room. Immediately, I found my daughter and gave her a big hug. We were so glad to see each other!

It was freezing outside, and very late, and we were both extremely tired. Winter in Romania is bitterly cold. We spent some time looking for a taxi and found a few, but they were priced too high for Lindsey to feel good about taking them. So, we walked around and around in circles—cold, tired, and carrying three big suitcases. Eventually, we found ourselves back in front of the airport. At this point, after waiting so long in and around there, I thought we had thoroughly bonded with the airport. I wanted to take a video of it. I took out my movie camera and shot about a ten-second video of the front of the airport.

As I finished, three uniformed men came up and started speaking directly to us in Romanian. Lindsey has a limited but impressive skill in the Romanian language—considering the meager four months she had been there. She understood enough to tell me that the men were policemen and that it's against the law to take video pictures of the airport. One pointed, and sure enough, there was a little sign off in the distance—about the size of a quarter from where I was standing—of a video camera with an international red line through it. He started making motions with his hands indicating handcuffs and talking about my going to jail. Great!

I told Lindsey to tell him that I would be happy to give him the tape or to erase it. She tried to communicate my willingness to oblige, but they wouldn't be placated.

This wouldn't sound good in the best of circumstances, but I had been awake for thirty-six hours, I was terribly tired, and I was having trouble focusing, standing in the dead cold of a Romanian winter—and these men were talking about throwing me in jail!

When all appeared completely hopeless, it dawned on Lindsey that they wanted a bribe. The corruption of Romania is replete. Teachers are paid to give their students A's. Surgeons and nurses are bribed to give good treatment to their patients. Policemen are bribed to avoid taking people to jail. Lindsey reached in her pocket and pulled out what looked like a small fortune—turned out it was only $5 or so in U.S. currency—and gave it to the head policeman.

The second the money was transferred into his hands, he stopped making the handcuff gestures, stopped talking about taking me to jail, and told me I could keep the videotape. He then offered to get us transportation to our hotel. You'd have thought he was our best friend in the world! He found us a driver, and we loaded our suitcases into the airport shuttle.

Lindsey said, "Dad—welcome to Romania!"

Smiles all around, we headed for the warm hotel and a short but welcome night's sleep.

I learned two vital details on this exciting trip. Be sure to leave time for international connections longer than suggested—and always have extra cash when visiting Romania.

Stephen W. Houghtaling was born in Utah and raised in the Northwest. He graduated from Brigham Young University and Baylor College of Dentistry. He served a two-year mission for his church to Concepcion, Chile. He is a husband, father of three, and grandfather of five.

Dr. H. practiced dentistry in Astoria, Oregon, but is now retired and enjoys riding his Goldwing and watching his grandchildren's antics. He is calm and cheerful and looks on the bright side of everything. If the office were to catch on fire, he would say unexcitedly, "Now line up and follow me, everyone, and do be careful not to trip as we exit." His successor, S. Aaron Smith, has the same calm personality and is happily filling in for Dr. H.

"Please don't leave me. Please don't put me back in the cage."

Cat

Elizabeth Hayes

How did this happen? How did I end up with this cat?

For those of you who are cat-lovers, you might think these odd questions. Well, here's the thing—I have never been a cat lover!

I have always seen cats as elusive creatures who own their owners. I have shaken my head at this oddity and said, "No cats for me. Give me a dog—a dog who loves me, a dog who will run on the beach with me and snuggle up on the bed at night."

I want some gratitude and companionship for my efforts—not an ungrateful cat that goes about her way and is completely unimpressed with humans. So, how *did* this happen? How *did* I get this cat? The story unfolds slowly.

My niece, Jodi, works in a vet clinic where they have a cat adoption program. I was looking at the clinic's Facebook page and saw an exquisite black and white cat. Huge and exotic green eyes stared at me. White fur wrapped around her neck like a little ruff. Long whiskers stood out like tiny, waxed, white wires. On her nose was a small white dot—slightly off-center—and a speck of white fur sat below her lip.

She was a knockout—as far as cats go. I remember thinking, *That cat will go to a new home in no time at all.*

A couple months later, I was visiting with my niece, and she mentioned the cat adoption program. I asked what happened to the little black and white tuxedo cat.

"You mean Sammy?" Jodi asked.

"Yes, I think so," I answered.

My niece proceeded to tell me that Sammy was still at the clinic. It seemed she was very shy. When clients came in to select a cat, they were attracted to those arresting green eyes and would immediately ask to see her, but Sammy would quickly dart under her blanket in the cage. She would disappear from their sight, and they would move on to other cats who knew how to "strut their stuff." Jodi also noted that the kittens would usually go quickly, but grown-up cats, like Sammy, would remain—passed over, again and again.

I inquired about her several times over the following months. Sammy had become very sad and even more reclusive. I certainly was not interested in taking her but said I would ask around to see who might want a cat. I talked to friends and colleagues. No one was interested in taking the little one.

I found myself becoming annoyed—and a bit protective. How could they not want the small black and white ball of fur with those green eyes? What was wrong with them?

Then, the plea came out on Facebook:

> "Please consider fostering this little one. She has been in our clinic for over a year and is showing signs of distress. We are sure those signs will go away quickly, once she is in a good home."

I felt a sting in my heart. I began to worry. *Someone has to take this cat!*

There were a lot of responses:

> "My cat doesn't like other cats."
> "We have too many other cats."
> "She is beautiful, but..."
> "I would take her in a heartbeat, but..."

I was growing to dislike the word "but." The more I read the responses, the more irritated I became. Out of all those professed cat-lovers, I was hearing excuse after excuse. I began to worry that no one was going to rescue the little cat. I went to bed and tossed and turned, always envisioning her in that cramped cage, overwhelmed by the noises—becoming more and more despondent, her big green eyes glowing with desperation and loneliness.

My niece came to visit that week, and I asked her about Sammy. She said the cat's appetite was waning, and that she was hiding away under her blanket for hours and hours. Jodi added that she had taken Sammy out of the cage to hold her, and when she went to put her back, Sammy had reached out with one paw and touched Jodi's hand. She'd locked those big green eyes on her as if to say, "Please don't leave me. Please don't put me back in the cage. Stay with me." I felt that heart sting again, and my eyes filled with tears.

I heard this voice from nowhere say, "Well, someone has to step up to the plate for this cat. I'll take her! I will foster her."

I looked around to see who had said that. *It was me!* I slapped my face. What was I thinking? I am not a cat person. I don't know the first thing about cats. I wondered if I had lost my mind. Temporary insanity!

So, that is how Sammy came to join me. I had absolutely no intention of keeping her. I was just doing a good deed. I'd find a great home for her on the coast and get back to my normal life. I laughed at the thought of me—the cat hater—fostering a cat. But it would soon be over.

I quickly realized Sammy was afraid in her new foster home. She made the bedroom her safe place. She would hide under the bed.

As Sammy grew a bit more confident, she would rest on top of the bed. When I would enter the room, she would leap off—as if the bed were on fire—and skitter off to that safe, dark place. If I walked by when she was in her litter box, she would jump straight up into the air and let out a shrill, "B-r-r-r-r-r." Then, off she would scamper to her dark safe place.

One afternoon, I was surprised to see Sammy sitting on the window seat in my den. She saw me, let out a yelp, and ran to her safe place. I began to realize she needed a safe home where she could learn to trust, relax, and be happy. Good grief, what had I gotten myself into?

In time, Sammy made her home on top of the bed—still racing away when I walked in. At meal time, she would venture as far as the bedroom door and begin to talk to me as I fixed and brought her food. She made soft, quizzical little mews that made me smile. As time went on, she would come all the way out and walk back with me to where I placed her dish—all the while talking to me in those soft mews.

When I came home very late one evening, Sammy met me at the door with her green eyes blazing.

MEOW! MEOW! "Where have you been?" she seemed to ask. "You are late and I was worried! You are supposed to be at home here with me!" She whirled around me in circles—all the while, chastising me for my tardiness.

When I went to bed that night, Sammy bounced up on the bed beside me, laid her tiny, graceful head on my chest, and began to purr.

It's been three years, and Sammy—now Samantha—is still with me. She won't be going anywhere. *This* is her forever home. This little one stalked her prey, crept into my heart, and left her paw prints. I have been captured, and there is no possibility of being released.

Good grief—I'm a cat person!

"...he reached in his pocket
and pulled out a gun..."

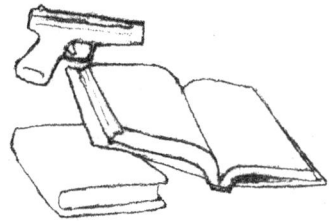

Incident at Walter's Cove

Nancy Carruthers

I am not an adventurous person. I'd rather be a spectator to other people's adventures, and so, our only real adventure came about unintentionally.

The summer of 1989, some friends invited us to accompany them on a boat trip around Vancouver Island, British Columbia, Canada. Our two boats would travel together, and since this would be a long trip, we took a lot of books with us.

In early June, my husband, Richard, and I met our friends in the island's port town of Nanaimo and started our cruise up the Pacific Coast's Inside Passage. The adventure began after we rounded the top of the island and started south again. Then we found ourselves on the wild side!

The west side of Vancouver Island is a wilderness—miles of unbroken rainforests growing to the top of rocky cliffs dropping down to the sea. Each night, we had to find safe anchorage in some little bay or cove, which would give us some protection from the ocean swells.

By then, we were beginning to realize our trip would continue in a new context—an alternate reality almost. The date, the day of the week, deadlines, appointments, all became meaningless.

Instead, our lives would be about knowing our location, the action of the tide, the barometer reading, the weather, the state of the sea, the number of hours until dark, and our next safe anchorage or place to take on fresh water.

It was also dawning on us how far we were from civilization. When we looked out to sea, we saw nothing. When we looked toward shore, we were looking at rocky cliffs and hundreds of square miles of impenetrable rain forest—with no human presence. We seldom saw another boat.

This was the real essence of our West Coast adventure—being exposed to the utterly different lifestyles of the few self-sufficient people living here on the edge of civilization and coping with the elements, the presence of wild animals, and the wilderness.

About halfway down the island, we found an interesting-looking small inlet on our chart called Walter's Cove. We decided to go there.

As we entered the cove, we were amazed to see civilization! On the one shore, there was a whole row of houses like the ones seen in any small town.

In the middle of the bay, there was a large high dock extending from shore with a ramp leading down to a float alongside for visiting boats to tie up to. We tied up and realized we were the only boat there.

Ashore we found a tiny general grocery store in the middle of the single row of houses. In front of the houses, along the top of the bluff, ran a wide dirt path, which the locals called Main Street. It was really beautiful!

That evening, Richard and I were sitting in the stern of our boat enjoying the stillness of the long twilight when I caught movement out of the corner of my eye. It was a pair of feet coming down the ramp. Our friends were not around.

When the feet got to the bottom of the ramp, we saw a young man standing there. Slowly, he started walking toward us. When he got alongside the boat, we exchanged greetings, and then, without invitation, he calmly stepped aboard.

This was most unusual.

As we began chatting, he told us he lived in Walter's Cove, and he had graduated from high school. When we asked about his future plans, he became vague. Then, he entered the interior of our boat and proceeded to the galley.

This was very strange, indeed!

Richard and I were feeling some alarm as we followed him and found him peering around the interior of the boat. He seemed especially interested in the row of books on the shelf over the dinette seat.

I asked him if he liked to read, and he answered, "Yes, but there aren't many books in Walter's Cove."

I realized later that was probably because there are no roads leading to Walter's Cove. The mail comes in on a helicopter, which lands on the dock.

I asked him what kind of books he liked to read. He was vague again. So, we mentioned some books we had recently read. Finally, my husband reached over, pulled a few books off the shelf, and spread them out on the table.

As the boy sat down to look at the books, he reached in his pocket and pulled out a gun, which he laid on the table beside the books.

We were suddenly hyper-alert.

The boy seemed nervous and hesitant. Richard and I concentrated on keeping our voices calm as we tried to carry on a conversation in a normal manner. As he began to look through the books, I asked him if he would like to take some home to read later—and to keep. He said that he would.

As he stood up, he casually put the gun back in his pocket and picked up the books. Then he calmly walked to the stern and exited the boat. What a relief it was to see him walking back up the ramp with his armload of books!

The next day, Richard and I found out the boy had shot and wounded the cove's mascot, Charley, the seal, who had been raised in a local bathtub. He got in trouble with the law for that, and also for some other things he'd done. Then it hit me. The reason for his trance-like demeanor had been because he was under the influence of drugs.

When we'd started the boat trip, who could have imagined our most exciting adventure would involve a juvenile delinquent suffering from book-deprivation! We'll never know what his intention was when he walked down to our boat that night.

We only know God was watching over us—and it was our books that saved the day.

"He would write of their fear,
their pain, their laughter..."

Ernie Pyle

Michael McCusker

Dago Mac was a reporter, marine combat correspondent, rifleman, and eyewitness. His job, as he saw it, was to be with the infantry, the self-styled grunts who lived, killed, and died in the mud and swill like pigs. He was one of a long line of United States Marine Corp journalists that ostensibly began reporting on the beach at Guadalcanal Island in World War II.

During the Vietnam War, Dago made a dramatic gesture while on Okinawa, waiting to be shipped "down South" to Vietnam. He hired a small boat and went out to the tiny island of le Shima, where he knew he would find a special monument.

Ernie Pyle, a Pulitzer Prize winning, WWII war correspondent, had been killed on le Shima by Japanese machine gun fire in the last and one of the bloodiest campaigns of the war he so eloquently reported on. Pyle was loved by the soldiers because he wrote about them from their vantage—taking their risks and suffering their discomforts. He loved them in return.

After his death, President Harry S. Truman said Pyle "told the story of the American fighting man as the American fighting men wanted it told." No newspaperman had ever been as close to, or written so plaintively and eloquently of, the common soldier who bears the weight of all wars.

He was called "The Little Man's Little Man" in a book by another reporter. He was a small, frail man with a long, thin head, and he was always terrified.

Somehow, he found it in himself to go where the soldiers went, and at the end, he was with the Army's 305th Infantry Regiment of the 77th "Liberty Patch" Division on le Shima.

Dago found the monument. It was smaller than he had expected. He'd thought it would be on a hill instead of in a small, undistinguished valley. It was a stone marker, which had replaced an original hand-lettered sign, and a later marker, but the words were the same:

AT THIS SPOT
THE 77TH INFANTRY DIVISION
LOST A BUDDY
ERNIE PYLE
18TH APRIL 1945

Dago might have knelt if he'd not thought it unseemly. He stood instead with his hands clasped as if in church. He made a promise that was more like a prayer. He promised to do what Pyle had done. He promised to stick with the grunts and write their stories, no matter how scared and cowardly he felt. He promised that though he might be of no other use, when the "s**t hit the fan," he would write honestly and lucidly of the men he honored. He would write of their fear, their pain, their laughter, their irreverence, and their desperate prayers for continued life. He would love them, defend them, and stick with them through the worst. Most of all, he prayed he would keep his promise.

Dago Mac kept most of his promises. He stuck with the grunts and saw and did things he wished he'd never been a part of. He learned to hate the grunts as much as he loved them. He hated their frail humanity that made them behave like savage animals. He hated their cruelty, their viciousness, and their hatred and contempt for the Vietnamese. He hated himself for being indistinguishably one of them—and for his indisputable loyalty to them.

"I didn't think it was that deep!"

A Hunting We Will Go

Bud Yardley

I think you could say I've always been interested in hunting and fishing because that was the culture I grew up in. My Dad and his friends always hunted and fished, so I knew when I was old enough, I'd have my turn.

The first hunting trip I remember was with my Dad, Fred Yardley. I was probably five or six years old, and at that time, we lived in Leesville, Louisiana. He took me deer hunting in the swamps. It was during WWII, and having meat to eat was unheard of at that time.

Dad carried a pump-22 with an octagon barrel, and he said, "We have to be real quiet." That was so hard for me because I was really excited, but Dad was patient.

He said, "You've got to shoot the deer in the eye so as not to waste the meat and have a clean kill."

I can still see that deer looking at us when it fell dead. We shared the meat with our neighbor, who had two boys about my age.

****

At the coast, pheasant season opened at noon. We were each allowed three male birds. Dad and I were walking back to the truck, heading for home with our limits. A game warden we knew well, and who also lived in Warrenton, Oregon, was standing by the pickup, and he wanted to see our birds. We laid them on the tailgate, and he said, "It looks like you have one too many."

I looked at him like he was nuts. There were only six birds on that tailgate. He laughed and pointed at Dart, my dog. Dart had found a cripple and had carried it back to the truck. The game warden asked if he could take the bird from Dart.

I gulped and told him, "Help yourself."

When we got home, we all had a good laugh at that one.

****

In 1956, Mom, Dad, and I went to Missouri on vacation. We visited some of Dad's relatives and went out to the old Yardley home place. It was in the Ozarks.

Uncle Bill Black wanted to go squirrel hunting. Dad had brought my .22 with us.

Uncle Bill said, "You're only supposed to shoot the squirrel in the head, and don't waste any of the meat."

I was the only one who killed anything.

On the way home, I was sitting in the back of the truck, and I asked Dad to give me my canteen of water. He handed it out the window to me. I took a drink and just reached around and dropped it in Uncle Bill's lap. He was driving down the old road, and he just opened the door and jumped out.

Dad grabbed the wheel, but we were already off the road and into the brush. Dad got the truck stopped, and we ran back to see if Bill was okay. I didn't know it, but Uncle Bill had been shell-shocked in the war, and he thought I'd dropped a hand grenade in his lap. I really felt bad about that.

****

A year later, back in Warrenton, my friend, Ronald Teague, and I were going deer hunting one morning. We got an early start, and as we were going down a logging road before daylight, we caught a nice buck crossing the road in the headlights of the pickup. I pulled over next to it. It just stood beside the truck. Ronald always carried a pistol, and I asked him to hand it to me. I rolled the window down and was pointing the pistol at the deer's ear when I felt a tap on my shoulder.

I looked around, and Ron whispered, "Here's the shell."

The deer took off like a flash. We just sat there and laughed until it hurt. At least we didn't have a loaded gun in the pickup.

****

Dad, Ronald, and I were duck hunting along the backwater of the bay front.

Ron and I were on the far side of the slough when Dad arrived on the other side and asked, "How'd ya get over there?"

"We waded across," Ron told him.

"How deep is it?" Dad asked.

Ron started to say something, when Dad stepped off the bank into the water and sank in over his head. I remember standing there stunned, watching his brimmed hat floating away from the spot he went down. Then, before we could move, he came up, threw his gun on the bank, and climbed out of the slough yelling at us about how deep it was as he took off one boot after the other and dumped the water out of them.

"I didn't think it was that deep," Ronald hollered back across the slough. "I just saw a duck walk across, and it only came up to his belly."

Dad grumbled some more and told us he'd meet us at the truck. Ron and I looked at one another and seriously considered whether it might not be better to walk home.

****

Early one morning, Dad and I went deer hunting. It was before daylight, and I was driving. I came around a curve in the road, and there stood a nice buck. I stopped with the headlights shining on him. Dad rolled the window down, stuck his gun out, and pulled the trigger. Snap went the gun, and off ran the deer.

I was laughing at the look on Dad's face when he

realized he hadn't loaded a shell in the chamber. He set the butt of the rifle on the floor, pulled back the bolt, and slammed a shell into the chamber. The gun went off and blew a hole in the roof of my truck's cab. That's probably why I don't hear very well out of my right ear to this day.

****

One of my favorite fishing stories is about the time Dad and I were drifting down the Wilson River in my boat. Dad had never caught a steelhead, and that day, the water was just right, and the weather was good.

I pulled into a stump hole and told Dad to cast up above the stump and raise the end of his pole. Then, when the line was even with the stump, he should drop the end of his rod so the bait would go under the roots. I saw his pole begin to dip on the end, and I knew he had one on his line.

I said, "Are you going to let it eat the end of your pole off, or are you going to set the hook?"

Dad jerked on his pole, and the fight was on. He finally got the fish close to the boat so I could net it. We got the steelhead into the boat, and Dad was beaming from ear to ear. I held his catch up by the head and tail for him to look at. It weighed about twelve to fifteen pounds and was a really nice fish.

He was sitting there looking at it and smiling when I said, "You don't want this old thing," and threw it overboard.

When we got home, Dad told Mom and my wife, Marlene, they were lucky I'd been allowed to come home with him. Why did I let his first steelhead go? Just orneriness, I guess.

****

For several years, a friend of mine, Champ Church, encouraged me to put in for a moose permit in eastern Idaho. That spring, I took Champ seriously and thought moose hunting would be fun and something Marlene and I could do together. After tossing the idea around, we decided to put in for the once-in-a-lifetime group permit. We had friends who had applied for years and hadn't been successful, so we felt our chances of drawing a permit were extremely slim.

In early May 2002, Marlene and I received letters from Idaho Fish and Game saying, "Congratulations!" and each envelope contained a bull-moose permit. Now, the real planning began. We checked out the area and started target practice. The season opened August 30. For nine days, we rode our all-terrain vehicles up and down the trails of some of the most beautiful country in Idaho. We saw many cows and calves, but no bulls. The locals were extremely friendly and offered advice as to where to find the best moose country.

They told us, "Come back about the middle of October when it gets a little colder."

We returned to the area on October 18th. On the evening of October 19th, while riding our ATVs down a canyon, enjoying the beautiful fall colors, we saw two bulls 100 yards up the hillside and approximately fifty yards apart. I told Marlene to take the one in the open, and I'd take the one near the timber.

With my 300-Weatherby rifle, I fired a shot, hitting my bull behind the ear. I heard the thwack of a solid hit, which broke his neck, and down he fell.

With Marlene's Ruger-M77 Magnum rifle, she hit her bull, too. He stumbled around and attempted to move down the hill. Another shot, and again, I heard the thwack of a solid hit, and he went down. When the shouting was over, reality set in.

I asked Marlene, "What have we done?"

We had two moose to clean before dark and we were eight and a half miles from the pickup. We knew we'd have to get into town to call our son and son-in-law for help hauling the moose out. We were thankful we had kids who would realize their parents needed to be rescued. Marlene and I had a good laugh about how the wheel goes around. A few years before, we'd had to rescue the kids, and that night would be payback time.

We had to field dress both bulls, which involved Marlene literally crawling inside of each moose to remove the entrails. Their hearts were as big as footballs, and their lungs were huge—almost the size of inner tubes. My bull weighed 1,150 pounds field dressed, with a thirty-six-and-one-quarter-inch rack spread. Marlene's bull weighed 1,400 pounds field dressed, with a thirty-six-inch rack spread. We suddenly knew why they only give you one moose permit in a lifetime—it would take a lifetime to eat all that moose meat!

By the time we'd finished, it was dark, so we covered the moose and headed back to the truck so we could get to town and call the kids to come help. I was puzzled when Marlene took off and left me in her dust. I followed her back to the truck, and once there, I asked her why she'd been in such a rush.

In the light from the truck's headlights, Marlene told me to look at her and said emphatically, "We're in bear country, and look at me. I'm covered in blood!"

When we got into town and contacted our son, he commented, "You mean you didn't hang up the carcasses?"

Marlene and I looked at each other in sheer disbelief, and I responded, "Oh, sure. Your mom and I—just the two of us—hung up those horse-size carcasses."

At the Ranger Station, after we checked our moose and gathered all the needed information, the Fish and Game officer commented, "You two should buy a lottery ticket!"

Bud Yardley was a 1959 graduate of Warrenton High School in Warrenton, Oregon. In the US Army, he was stationed in Albuquerque, New Mexico, on the Atomic Energy Base known as DASA. While there, he met, became best friends with, and married Marlene. Now retired, the two of them return to the Oregon coast every chance they get.

"As soon as I started opening the door,
I heard fierce growling."

Duchess Elkheart

Pat Williams

Late in the summer of 1978, shortly before our return to Oregon from Union Lake, Michigan, our boys, Aaron, age eleven, and Shawn, age eight, were out riding their bikes. As usual, they were in an off-limits area on the other side of a busy highway.

While playing with some other kids, they were joined by a half-grown puppy. She looked to be about half grown and only came up to my knee, but she had the appearance of a golden retriever. Now according to them, they started to come home, and the pup started following them. So, they did what all normal red-blooded boys would do. They headed home, followed closely by the pup. They stopped periodically and tried to chase her away, telling her to, "Go home!" but she just wouldn't leave them. As a result, they arrived home followed closely by this enthusiastic puppy.

Both boys knew that Bud—my husband and the father of our troop of five—had emphatically stated no more dogs. We'd just lost Taji, our three-year-old Russian wolfhound. She was supposed to be a family dog but was too hard for any of the kids or myself to handle, so she bonded with Bud, and he with her. Taji came to Michigan with us from Oregon when we'd moved in the spring of 1976.

Unfortunately, she escaped one afternoon and followed some high school kids down the street. Taji saw a nice place to run, took off, and ran into the side of a passing pickup truck. She had a serious head wound, and while the vet was telling us she might not make it, her heart went into defibrillation, and she was gone.

Although the rest of the family was really upset, Bud was devastated. I think it was the first time any of the kids had ever seen their dad cry—or any man crying. It really impacted the kids, especially the boys, as they'd grown up in a world that preached, "You've got to be tough. No crying!"

Because of this, all of us knew why Bud didn't want another dog right away, but that didn't stop the kids from wanting to help this apparently "lost" pup. Both boys pleaded with me to let them keep her while they tried to find her owner.

Since Bud was out of town for the week, I weakened and said, "Sure, but you've got to find her home before we leave for Oregon next month."

This started the weirdest month ever. Shawn got the pup so good at hiding from Bud, he never realized we had a dog in residence. In the meantime, the boys enlisted their sisters, and all the neighbor kids, to try to find the puppy's home. They made posters and put them up all over the place. With the pup on a leash, they went door-to-door asking if anyone knew her or knew where she belonged. As the days ticked by, the kids and I got more and more attached to the happy little pup. At the same time, we were all getting more and more desperate, because we just couldn't find anyone who knew the dog.

I finally figured out where the boys had been the day they'd found her, when they begged me to take them farther and farther from our home in the search. It was mid-August when they first came home with her following behind, and by then it was the first week of September. The movers had already come, taken all our belongings to Oregon, and placed them in storage until we got there. We'd bought a used tent trailer to use for the trip west. The kids were sleeping in the trailer in front of the house, and Bud and I were using sleeping bags and an air mattress in the living room.

Every night before heading to bed, I'd walk around the trailer, making sure everything was secure and the kids were asleep. One night, I got ready for bed and then realized I hadn't checked on the kids.

When I grumbled about it, Bud said, "No problem, I'll check tonight."

Without thinking about it, I said okay. He put his shoes on, grabbed the flashlight, and went out the front door. In just a couple minutes, he was back with a really strange look on his face.

He asked quite calmly, "So, where did the dog come from?"

I gulped and told him about the puppy and assured him the kids and I were doing everything we could to try to find the dog's owner.

Bud then grinned and casually commented, "Well, as far as I'm concerned, that dog can come with us to Oregon."

I was shocked!

I asked Bud why he'd decided that, and he told me, "When I went out to the trailer, I automatically opened the door to go in and check on the kids. As soon as I started opening the door, I heard fierce growling. I turned the beam in that direction and saw this little, half-grown dog spread out over the top of Shawn, covering as much of him as possible and growling ferociously at me—telling me, 'Stay back! This is my boy and you can't hurt him.' I figure, if the pup is that protective of him and the other kids at this age, it would be a good dog to have around."

I was so relieved at how it had all worked out. The kids kept looking for the pup's home as the time to our departure dwindled down. We'd decided we'd take her with us to Oregon if we couldn't find her owner before then, and the kids started calling her Duchess.

By the middle of September, we were really flagging it trying to get ready to get on the road. Bud was no longer working, so he could be home to help. Unfortunately, he had developed a severe reaction to the sun because of the blood pressure medication he was taking, so I was the one packing everything in the tent trailer and on the car top carrier of our 1970 Chevy Suburban.

Late one afternoon, I was up on top of a ladder putting stuff into the car top carrier when a car came slowly driving down our unpaved street. Suddenly, the pup jumped up from where she was lying and ran toward the car, tail wagging, whining in excitement.

The young woman driving the car stopped and jumped out crying, "Elke! Elke! Oh, baby! It's you!"

By the time I'd climbed down from the top of the ladder, she and the dog were a mass of squirming puppy and hugging woman.

I walked over and waited until she stood up, then commented, "It looks like you and your dog have found each other."

As I said it, my heart felt like a lead lump, and I was frantically trying to think of what to say to the kids. They'd tried so hard to find the puppy's owner, but after so much time, had begun to think of her as their dog.

The woman and I exchanged pleasantries, and then she asked how Elke had come to be with us. I told her the story of how the boys had found her, and then she told her side of things. Apparently, she'd gotten a new job and had to move, but she was unable to find an apartment that allowed dogs. So, she'd found Elke a new home with a friend—an unmarried woman with a couple kids. She'd left Elke there, feeling quite confident it would work out. However, what she didn't know was the woman had a boyfriend who had no patience and a nasty temper. When Elke got into the garbage, he'd taken a broomstick to her and beaten her unmercifully. She'd run away, never to return.

Her friend finally told her what had happened and that even if Elke could be found, she wouldn't be able to keep her. Her boyfriend wouldn't have a "garbage" dog in the place. The young woman explained that she was terribly upset and had been frantically looking for Elke everywhere, every chance she could get back to Union Lake. She had tears in her eyes as she reached down and petted Elke. She finished by saying she was so terribly happy to find her alive and well.

By the time we'd shared our stories, my kids had congregated around us—looking upset. I think we were all waiting for the woman to say, "Well, thanks for finding my dog. I should just take her and go now."

Instead, we were amazed when she asked, "There isn't any chance you would like to keep Elke, is there? I've been looking, but I just can't find a place that will let me have her, and none of my friends can take her."

Instantly, I had five pairs of anxious eyes pleading with me. I knew Bud's feelings and mine were similar, so without missing a beat, I answered, "Sure, we'd love to have her! But, as you can see, we're in the process of moving—in fact, all the way out to Oregon."

Her response was positive. "Really? Oh, I'm so glad. I'll miss her, but I'm so pleased she'll have a family of her own. Thank you. Thank you so much!"

We talked for a few more minutes—then she was gone, and the pup was ours. The kids all decided her name should be Duchess Elkheart, but we'd call her Elke for short. Elke came to Oregon and lived a long life, well loved by all of us. Her life ended the summer of 1988, just after our youngest, Shani, graduated from high school. By then, there was just Bud, Shawn, Shani, and myself living at home to hug Elke and shed tears at her death. She left a huge hole in all our lives and is still sorely missed. So many of our favorite family memories include Elke, who grew up to retain her golden retriever looks, but in a much smaller body.

When Shawn died in 2006, I couldn't help but think of him being greeted in heaven by all those special people who'd gone on before him, but especially by one excited, wiggling puppy who'd been waiting for her special boy.

"A network of lines and patterns,
an enormous abandoned sketchpad..."

A Network in Nazca

Brian F. Harrison

On my way to Cahuachi, Peru, an archaeological project in the desert, I had a plan to hire a flight over the famous Nazca Lines. There had been no time on my previous visits, and this was a determined goal.

From Lima, I took the seven-hour bus ride south on the Pan-American Highway, passing the towns marking the occasional river flowing down from the Andes to the sea, towns with exotic names: Chincha, Pisco, Paracas, Ica, Palpa, and finally, Nazca.

After hours of empty sand dunes, I forgot my intention to carefully observe everything we passed. My mind wandered, and I only woke from my reverie when we passed the dusty adobe towns. Signs for gasoline, tire repairs, chicken and rice, and Cristal beer bracketed the tan buildings with color and life, while children, goats, and dogs roamed the streets—feral and unkempt.

Late in the evening, we arrived in Nazca, where the bus was swarmed by agents of the local hotels, and more taxis than seemed warranted for a town this size. The emissaries were shoving one another to get to the passengers, catching our eyes with brochures for hotels and tours, grabbing our luggage, hoping we would be dazed enough to comply with their frenetic urging.

I selected a woman with long black hair who spoke a bit of English and had a list of hotels ranked by number of stars. Maria led me to a taxi, which took me to a hotel, but when I looked at the offered room, the three stars turned out to be an imaginary rating.

Walking down the dark street to another motel that looked newer and cleaner, I rented a windowless room, like a monk's cell, with a single bed and one caned chair. At least it had its own bathroom and a lock on the door. I also signed up and paid for a plane flight in the morning, requesting a receipt for my $50, hoping Maria hadn't taken me for an expensive ride.

During the long bus trip south, I ate two granola bars for lunch. And now, in Nazca, I was hungry, but the food available around the hotel was dirty and undercooked.

In searching for restaurants, I had passed through the central plaza. On a high stand in the park, like an altar at a shrine, was a television set showing *Swan Lake* to twenty or thirty people, rapt in their attention to the Russian fantasy. As I sat on a bench watching the Nazcans watching the ballet, I was approached by several boys asking if they could shine my sandals, and if not, could they have a souvenir from the United States—perhaps a dollar bill.

The Hotel Mirador was clean, though I thought $35 a night was a way to gouge tourists visiting the famous lines. The one glass in the bathroom was lipstick-smeared and crusted with something brown, but I needed a drink. I washed it with hot tap water, rinsed it with bottled water, and poured in brandy—and assumed it was more or less sterile from this treatment.

The bed was too small, but I slept well, dreaming about foxes, and whales, and pelicans on the great pampas.

Truck rumbles and taxi horns were my wake-up call, and I was ready for breakfast at seven. The hotel's idea of breakfast was a stale roll with jam and a cup of instant coffee. Maria had told me to be ready at 8:00 a.m. on the dot, and I was, but she arrived in a taxi to tell me there was too much fog and she'd return for me in an hour.

At 9:00 a.m., she returned and said the planes were still not flying, and she would pick me up at 10:30 a.m., for sure. By noon, she hadn't returned, and I was getting hungry and frustrated. I growled when she finally picked me up for the ride to the airport. She signed me in with the woman who was keeping the first-come logbook and told me it would be a twenty-minute wait.

I spent the next two hours waiting, until at 2:00 p.m., an Italian woman and I browbeat the poor logbook woman into writing our own names on the next passenger manifest.

The Cessna small plane took off without incident, and our pilot, Alejandro, gave us a thrilling half-hour in the air.

Flying over the arid pampas of southern Peru, suspended over the rocks and sand, there's nothing between my head and the ground but a thin sheet of glass and a thousand feet of desert air. Alejandro turns the Cessna on edge, wings pointing to sky and earth instead of a sensible horizontal attitude. He loops the plane around so the other passenger can look straight down. My stomach, which had shifted to the right, is now sagging left and protesting.

The object of these maneuvers is visible below: a monkey with big ears, a spider of perfect symmetry, a delicate humming bird, a "spaceman" with hand raised in greeting, trapezoids like wide landing fields, lines laser-straight five miles across the rocky uneven terrain, and a condor with a football-field wingspan. A network of lines and patterns, an enormous abandoned sketchpad with triangles, double spirals, animals, trees, and flowers, are etched into the rocky desert pavement. A blacktop highway bisects some of the lines, and here and there, two-lane tracks carelessly cross a figure, destroying the grace and artistry of the ancient drawings.

I might as well have used black and white film, the lunar landscape being shades of gray. The markings are barely visible in the transparent light of early afternoon, light without shadow or form.

But, I shoot my color slides anyway, hoping to capture the mystery and forgotten meaning of the geoglyphs. A landing field for alien spacecraft? An astronomical observatory? A calendar for planting? A plat map of underground water sources? A meditative pathway? I have my own theory, but truth be told, nobody alive knows.

In the distance, there is fog in the lowlands to the west, flowing from one valley to the next, the intervening hills rising like islands above the clouds. Alejandro soars over one last figure then returns to the airport north of town. After the sea of gray, the fields and buildings are a fragment of rainbow. I had waited for the experience for a year and a half. Six hours later, it is over, like a dream.

When we landed, I walked to the highway and got a taxi into town where a driver was waiting in his copper-colored '79 VW beetle to take me to Cahuachi.

At the maligned Hotel Mirador, when I walked in to pick up my suitcase and pay my bill, I was startled to find it was thirty-five *nuevos soles*, not dollars. So, for a $12 hotel room, I stopped complaining.

After a bowl of goat stew, I finished my trek to the desert site of Cahuachi. I had satisfied my desire to see the lines from the air and compare the reality with all the books I had read. I still didn't understand the geoglyphs, or why they were constructed 2,000 years ago, but I had seen them with my eyes, and that was enough for now.